THE GOLDEN BOWL

THE GOLDEN BOWL

by

ARCHIE JOSCELYN

WILDSIDE PRESS

www.wildsidebooks.com

"TO MY MOTHER"

CHAPTER I

"Ah, Mr. Hearle, the famous detective? I'm so thrilled to meet you. Do you know, Mr. Hearle, I've often wondered—perhaps you can tell me? Doesn't a detective's presence at such a party as this, somehow infer that a crime is to take place before that party is ended?"

Eric Hearle smiled dryly. He was a tall, slightly stooping man of about middle age, with dark hair faintly silvered, and very blue eyes which always looked slightly puzzled, as though by life itself. He regarded the woman before him attentively, while not appearing to do so. She was a brunette of the type known as willowy, perhaps thirty-five, or even more, though striving by every means known to modern art to look at least ten years younger; strikingly beautiful once, Hearle decided, and very good looking still, though she would have been much better had she been content to accept the years rather than to fight against their march.

"I trust not," Hearle replied. "I should feel myself always to be a sort of Jonah, if that were so, and it would, I'm afraid, be a most unpleasant sensation."

Mrs. Reid smiled slightly. She was a widow, Eric Hearle had gathered, though of just what degree, he had not learned.

9

"But don't you detectives just love crimes, so that you can have something to do? I've always understood that you were happiest when running a criminal to earth. Like bloodhounds, you know."

Hearle shrugged wearily.

"I've never felt that way about it," he contradicted. "At the present time, I'm on a vacation, and I sincerely trust that nothing will turn up to spoil it."

"Oh, I do hope that we have a first-class murder or something, though," Mrs. Reid retorted. "And I'm sure we will."

Hearle cocked one eyebrow interrogatively.

"You have advance information, perhaps?"

"Oh, mercy, no. It's just a—a feeling. Some of my friends tell me I'm psychic."

"The damp air, perhaps—" Hearle was beginning, with a smile that took the sting out of his words, when the door to the suite opened again, to admit three newcomers. Hearle turned to them with relief. He had been the first guest to arrive that evening, had been ushered into a sitting room by Gage, and left to his own devices, since his host had not yet shown up. Mrs. Reid had come shortly afterward.

Lon Leadley, the host, rushed forward now to greet his guests. Hearle felt that this young man, big, bronzed, a golden-haired god and popular movie star, public idol though he might be, was the genuine article, unspoiled and natural. He was a Helena product, Hearle remembered, had been

10

raised not far away on a Montana ranch, and when he posed as a cowboy in the films he knew his business. Perhaps this return to his native city made him feel like a boy just out of school; anyway, he acted the part.

"Mighty sorry not to have been here when you came, Mrs. Reid, and Hearle," he apologized. "Fact is, I was out to my ranch on the Dearborn— we're turning it into a dude ranch, you know— and I had two punctures on the way back. Delayed us a little. Miss Sargent, permit me to introduce Eric Hearle, the famous detective. Richard Sargent, Eric Hearle. A great stroke of luck, really, for me to be able to persuade Mr. Hearle to join our party for a few days. Though I think that I can promise you all a real vacation, out at the ranch."

Hearle, as he acknowledged the introductions, was studying the newcomers with more than passing interest. Richard Sargent was a man of perhaps forty, medium in build, quiet, unobtrusive, yet with a forceful, distinguished personality that nothing could hide. His daughter, Joan, was all that Mrs. Reid desired to be and could not.

A gust of rain rattled against the windows; outside, a confused drone came up from the street, the sounds of motor cars, a distant locomotive whistle. Inside the hotel an elevator door clanged, some voice spoke sharply, was lost as a door closed; a snatch of music floated like a wraith upon the air, was gone again.

By now, the other guests were arriving rapidly, crowding into the room. Louis Jouralmon came next, a man of fifty—rather large, impressive, and,

11

like Sargent, a man of the world, largely traveled. His face was arrogantly handsome, a mask from behind which the true emotions of the man seldom shone forth.

Closely following him came the Misses Ferguson—Elinor and Margaret, twins, blonde, svelte and beautiful. Their father, the Senator, had been detained in Washington, but was leaving that day to join the party—was due to arrive on Thursday, Hearle understood.

John Kasmin was ushered in, and talked rather loudly, boisterously, plainly ill at ease and clumsily seeking to hide it. How did he come to be among Leadley's guests? Hearle wondered, studying him. A powerful figure, with something ruthless in his face; past fifty, dark, too flashily dressed, with too much jewelry; obviously desirous of pleasing, but certainly out of place. Then, last to arrive, Pinard, Leadley's famous director—silent behind a saturnine smile, eminently proper in a devil-may-care way; and with him, Dolores Dixon, Leadley's leading woman, a star in her own right, flashing a bewitching smile to right and left, throwing a cheery greeting to everyone, ravishingly beautiful without make-up, dark, almost a Spanish type.

She was the outstanding character actress of them all, in Hearle's private opinion, an opinion in which a great many others shared. He had wondered about her before. Now he saw an indefinable quality which lurked behind her gayety—the hint of shadowing wings, of tragedy; here was no petty character, come to fame through a pretty face, accident and the art of a skilled director.

A servant quietly entered the room, moved to

12

the windows to close them against a fresh gust of rain, shutting out the noises of the night, bringing in an intimate coziness. Outside, the night had grown black already, despite the earliness of the hour. Hearle judged that it would rain most of the night.

His eyes followed the servant approvingly. Gage was an Englishman, a gray-haired man and faultless at his work. Leadley had picked him up at the beginning of his own career, five years before.

"Dinner is served, sir," Gage announced presently, throwing open the door to the dining room. Seated, Hearle found himself alone at the one end of the table, there being only eleven guests. Elinor Ferguson was on his right, Sargent on his left. Leadley himself, with Dolores Dixon, was at the other end of the table, the remaining guests grouped in between.

"The boy knows how to do things, doesn't he?" Sargent murmured approvingly. "This is the best suite of rooms in the hotel, and the Last Chance is easily one of the finest hotels in the north-west, he tells me. A likable boy."

Hearle concurred heartily. The meal began, served by waiters of the hotel who came and went noiselessly; the conversation was at a lively tempo, set chiefly by Leadley himself. Plainly, he was having a good time, and he took pains to see that all of his guests should have a good time as well. Dolores Dixon ably seconded him. Leadley was a perfect host; was he the perfect lover as well, even when not paid for it, Hearle wondered. Dolores seemed in no wise to resent it.

"I fancy," said Leadley suddenly, during a momentary lull in the conversation, "that it would be difficult to gather a more distinguished company than this, without increasing the number—always excepting myself, of course. But leaving out Miss Dixon here, and Pinard, the most famous director in Hollywood, look whom we have here: Mrs. Reid, Margaret Ferguson, Elinor Ferguson, Louis Jouralmon, Joan Sargent, Richard Sargent, John Kasmin—all world travelers, distinguished figures, not to mention Eric Hearle, internationally famous detective. I like to name over the list. Being host to such company makes me feel as if I amounted to something."

All joined in the laugh. The talk then turned to travel. It was plain that Jouralmon and Sargent were the most widely traveled of all.

"I think I've seen nearly every country on the face of the globe," Jouralmon remarked, "with the exception of the one that has always held the greatest interest for me."

"And what country is that?" demanded Mrs. Reid, who sat opposite Jouralmon.

"China — the Celestial Land," Jouralmon replied. "I've always had a curiosity about China, a desire to see it, and, as you might say about most of those Eastern countries, to smell it. I've tried more than once. But fate has always ordained otherwise."

"How is that?" Leadley asked. "It sounds as though you might have a story to tell."

"A dozen, if I wished," Jouralmon agreed. "But I won't bore you with details. Shipwreck intervened once. Once I tried to cross eastward from Siberia, but there was a mix-up about the passport—I was suspected of being some sort of plotter against the Czar's government—and though they couldn't prove it and hardly dared press it much, since I was an American citizen, they took me clear back across Siberia and Russia and set me down in Germany. I had been there before, if they had only thought to inquire."

He paused during the laugh which followed, then resumed:

"Sickness once caused me to be transferred to a boat which was better equipped medically. Another time I might have won out, but I was short of funds, and to keep from starving, had to take the only job I could get, which happened to be shipping on board a vessel bound for London. And so it went. China has eluded me. Though I still have hopes."

Hearle noted that Richard Sargent had been listening attentively, a peculiar light glowing in his eyes at the tale, a faintly sardonic smile flickering about his mouth. But now it was his turn, as his host urged him to talk.

But Sargent obviously did not care to talk. He passed it on to Hearle.

"I'm afraid that I won't shine very brightly in this traveled company," Hearle confessed. "My life has been more prosaic, stay-at-home, as you might say. Still, I seem to have been favored by fortune, and to have accomplished what Mr. Jouralmon failed to do. I've been in China."

"Oh, do tell us all about it, Mr. Hearle," Mrs. Reid gushed. "I'm just dying to hear of your adventures there."

15

"They didn't amount to much, personally," Hearle denied." Though I was on a rather interesting case—one of the most unusual that I have ever encountered during all my years as a detective, and the only one, I may add, that I failed flatly in—the only one that I ever had anything to do with that has never been solved, in any way, in all the succeeding years."

"That sounds interesting," Richard Sargent declared gravely. "Tell us more about it, please."

"It was about twenty years ago," Hearle began. "I was just starting out as a detective then, and was employed by a rather famous firm of detectives. We were hired on this case I have mentioned, and I was sent over with another member of the firm to try to work it out. But we failed.

"There wasn't, really, very much to go on. A man named Van Horn hired us—I may as well give his name, I suppose, since he and his brother both died many years ago. Van Horn and his brother, also his sister and her husband, whose name was Long, were all traveling in China. One day, the sister and her husband were found murdered, in an alley in the city of Shanghai.

"They had been lured there somehow or other—probably had been going somewhere, and their native guides had tricked them. They had been set upon by native thugs, done to death, robbed. Chinese daggers were the instruments used, I recall. Long had a good bit of money on him at the time, and she wore expensive jewelry. Robbery appeared to be the only motive."

He paused a moment. Everyone at the table

16

was watching him with strained attention, or so it seemed, engrossed in his narrative. Hearle went on.

"The brothers thought otherwise, however. That was why one of them hired my firm to investigate. There were some odd things connected with the case. The Van Horn fortune had been a large one—twenty millions, or thereabout, I believe. The elder Van Horn had died a few months before, and though leaving each son perhaps a half million, the bulk of his fortune had gone to the daughter, Mrs. Long. But there was one stipulation in the will. If she should die, without leaving descendants, the fortune was to go, not to her husband or to his family, but back to ,her brothers. So there was really some nineteen millions at stake."

"Goodness," whispered Mrs. Reid, audibly. "How thrilling!"

"Wasn't it?" Hearle agreed. "Well, as it developed, she did leave a baby daughter, only a few months old. It was found to have disappeared that same night, and for a while suspicion was cast upon her uncles, the Van Horn brothers. A little later, however, while they were still occupied in China, a sister of the murdered husband, Long—the girl's aunt, really—turned up in the United States with the baby. They—I say they, because the sister also had a husband, named Tinley—had a lot of money back of them,—and influence. They proved without difficulty that the child was the legal heir to the fortune, had themselves appointed guardian and custodian of the estate, got hold of it—all of this before the Van Horns, in China,

17

really got wind of what was going on, or had a chance to protest.

"Of course, it was all perfectly legal, so long as the Van Horns did not protest the guardianship, and this they had no chance to do. By the time they found out about it, the Tinleys and the baby had disappeared again. The Van Horn who had hired me spent a year then in trying to locate the baby or the Tinleys. He failed, as I understand, to find even a trace of them. They were always traveling, in some remote corner of the world.

"A year later it was reported that Mrs. Tinley was dead—had been found murdered under mysterious circumstances. But her husband and the child had disappeared. With them went the Van Horn millions. So far as I know, neither Tinley nor the baby has ever been heard of since. And the mystery that I was hired to solve, as to who did it and what it was really all about, is as big a mystery today as it was twenty years ago."

CHAPTER II

Tense silence held the room for a moment. The hotel servants had cleared the table, leaving only coffee, and departed. Leadley laughed a little to clear the tension.

"That case certainly had some of the out-of-the-ordinary aspects, all right," he declared. "But, since it's so long closed, we may as well come down to the present now. I have arranged a little entertainment for you tonight, which I think you will all enjoy. The lights will presently be flashed off, for a few moments only. Then they will go on again, and you all want to be looking your pleasantest, for when they go on again, a movie camera will be grinding.

"After it catches our expressions, the film will be developed, and we will have an opportunity to view ourselves on the screen before we retire for the night. Not that there's such a thrill left in that for Miss Dixon or myself, but some of you may enjoy it, and I'll be glad to have the record of so distinguished a company."

Gage came in, as staidly correct as ever, a small movie camera in one hand, a tripod in the other, and tried adjusting the machine at one end of the room. After a moment's experimenting, however, he moved it to the opposite end, near where Eric Hearle sat, but to his left. Having it adjusted to his satisfaction, Gage departed again, to return with

19

a small stand which he set up close at hand. Just behind him was a switch for turning the lights on and off.

"If you are all ready, ladies and gentlemen," he intoned, "why, the lights will be off only a few moments."

John Kasmin half-arose from his chair, protest written on his face.

"Is it necessary—?" he began, then shrugged, sat down again. "Oh, well, go ahead. Don't mind me. Nothing to worry about."

But Leadley was the perfect host.

"If you don't like it, old man, you've only to say the word," he insisted. "We don't aim to distress anybody."

Kasmin laughed shortly.

"Oh, I've had my picture taken before, and have been in the dark, too," he said. "Go ahead."

Leadley hesitated a moment, nodded to Gage.

"Oh, by the way," Leadley added. "Will everyone kindly remain in his place, please?"

The lights flashed off, leaving the room in pitch darkness. Eric Hearle remembered the expression on Kasmin's face in that last moment—rebellion, disgust, were there, despite his assurance that it was all right.

"May we talk?" It was Mrs. Reid's voice, nervous, uneasy, high-pitched.

"Of course," Pinard, beside her, replied smoothly. "This isn't a talkie record, but even if it was, we could talk the same as usual."

The moments dragged, endlessly. Soft stirrings, foot-falls, a hushed padding. A rattle of rain against the outer windows. Gage, muttering to himself. A soft humming, clicking noise, which Hearle decided was the movie camera, in operation. Leadley's voice, sharp above the muted noises.

"What's the trouble, Gage?"

"The lights won't seem to go on again, sir. I'll get them in a minute, though."

"Use your flash-light then, Gage. Give us some light."

"Yes sir. In just a moment, Mr. Leadley. Will everybody please keep his seat?"

Silence, broken by a muttered cursing. Someone was moving about. A tense air prevailed in the room. A broken sigh. Hearle expected someone to scream. And then, abruptly, the lights flashed on again.

As though drawn by a magnet, Hearle's eyes swept to Kasmin. He was still seated, as before the lights had gone out. But now he sagged forward over the table, arms resting upon it. One had tipped over his half-emptied coffee cup, the liquid of which had run to the edge of the table and was slowly dripping to the floor. His eyes were wide and staring, his face painfully contorted. Driven to the hilt from behind, its point in his heart, was a long, slim-bladed dagger.

This much Hearle noted in that first swift moment. Then his eyes ranged the rest of the table. Every guest was in place, seated as before, apparently quite calm. Gage stood now behind the camera, which was clicking steadily, running automatically through the pressing of a button. Nothing in the room seemed to be disturbed or out of order. No one else was present.

Eric Hearle was quickly on his feet, taking swift

21

command, keeping order by the dominance of his personality.

"Please keep your seats, everybody," he ordered. "Except as I instruct. Something has happened here, but we must be calm."

He made a swift scrutiny of every face about the table, but such emotions as showed now were only natural under the circumstances. Mrs. Reid sat staring at the dead man, her eyes large with horror, hand held over her mouth as though to repress a scream. Hearle walked swiftly about the room, then issued his orders.

"Leadley, notify the authorities. Pinard, Sargent, Jouralmon, please search this suite carefully, but go no further. No one is to leave these rooms at present. The rest of you may find other seats, but please do not disturb anything."

He moved, then, to Kasmin himself, and examined him carefully. Hearle saw at once that the dagger was long, slender, of Chinese origin, the handle inlaid with jade. It had plainly been driven by a sure and practised hand, from the back, one swift stroke that found the heart and killed instantly. The slain man had made no outcry, had scarcely moved, though Hearle remembered that heavy sigh. Only a drop or so of blood had welled out from the wound.

Hearle continued his examination, but nothing seemed to have been disturbed anywhere. Mary Yee, Miss Dixon's maid, was brought in from another room in the suite, where she protested that she had remained ever since the guests had begun to arrive. She was a pretty Chinese girl, American born, of about twenty-five, neat and efficient. No one else was hiding anywhere in the rooms, the searchers reported.

"Then all that we can do, at present, is to wait for the authorities," Hearle commented. Leadley added that they would be there very soon.

Almost at once, the coroner, Dr. Strait, and the sheriff, a Mr. Oliver, arrived. Leadley explained to them what had happened, introducing Eric Hearle.

"The famous detective, eh?" Dr. Strait inquired pleasantly. "I'm glad that you're here, Mr. Hearle. What do you make of it?"

"Nothing, so far," Hearle admitted. "He was murdered while the rest of us sat at a table with him. Killed instantly, I should say."

"Exactly," nodded the doctor. "A stroke like that, into the heart, could not fail to do so. I at once requested Sheriff Oliver to come with me," he explained, "because he is a finger-print expert, and from what Mr. Leadley said, it looked to me like a case for the county authorities rather than the local police. Though they, of course, have been notified."

At that moment, two policemen arrived. The door opened again, a moment later, to admit a rather serious young man whom Dr. Strait introduced as Critton, deputy county attorney.

"You folks seem to move quickly, out here," Hearle commented.

"I merely called them before coming myself," Dr. Strait nodded. "We've had one or two cases in the past that were badly bungled, and I thought it as well for the proper officials to be on hand at the start. Personally," he added, "it is my opinion that you should be given a free hand to investigate this case, Mr. Hearle. I presume that you will do so, and I may add that I have the utmost confidence in you."

"I will be glad to work with you, gentlemen, in any way possible," Hearle agreed.

The sheriff, carefully taking hold of the dagger, now withdrew it and wrapped it in his handkerchief. He straightened.

"My idea," he said, "is this: There's no need for us to duplicate each other's efforts, and merely get in the way. I propose that we each do the work that we are best adapted to. I can handle the finger-prints, and if there's anybody to be run down or arrested, I'll do my part there. For the regular investigation into the case, I think that Mr. Critton and Mr. Hearle should handle that end of it. Dr. Strait has his own duties, of course, and the police will be ready to do anything, or to cooperate with us, when called upon. Am I right?"

So it was agreed. Leaving the policemen to keep watch about the hotel, the sheriff and doctor presently departed. Critton turned to Hearle with a smile.

"I don't know much about this sort of thing, myself," he confessed. "That's why I like the idea of having an expert like yourself on the job. What do we do next?"

"There isn't much we can do until we hear what Mr. Oliver finds on that dagger," Hearle replied. "We can ask a few general questions tonight, but I fear that we won't get very far."

The body had been removed by now, the under-

24

taker had departed. Hearle called the guests together into the sitting room.

"Had any of you ever seen the dagger before?"
he asked.

Apparently no one had.

"Did any of you notice anything unusual while
the lights were out?"

But again, there was nothing but conjecture, and
having been present himself, Hearle knew all too
well the exact value of that.

"Have any of you anything to say that might
be of importance?" was his next query.

Again there was silence.

"Well," said Hearle, quietly, "since it is getting
late, that will be all for tonight. I believe that
you all have rooms in this hotel. Please do not
leave the hotel without telling either Mr. Critton
or myself first."

Most of them left the room rather hurriedly.
Critton expressed himself as disappointed.

"We don't seem to be learning anything this
way," he said. "And the murderer will have a
good chance to escape."

"True," agreed Hearle. "But reflect, my dear
sir. If it is anyone of this party, then they cannot
escape without throwing suspicion on themselves,
and in that case, we would quickly get them again.
We will begin our real investigation tomorrow. If
it was an outsider, as is entirely possible—for a
hotel employee, or almost anyone, familiar with the
room, could have slipped in, done the deed, and
out again—if it was an outsider, then they were
safely out and away before we had a chance to
even suspect, let alone apprehend them. I know of

25

no way to speed up their possible discovery. Do you?"

"That dagger should have finger-prints on it which will solve the whole thing," declared Critton.

"If so, fine," agreed Hearle. "Personally, I doubt it."

The phone rang. Hearle crossed to it.

"This is Oliver speaking," came the sheriff's voice. "I have gone over the dagger carefully, but it had evidently been wiped clean with a cloth, then held by gloved fingers or with a handkerchief. There's not even a trace of a finger-print on it."

"I didn't suppose there would be," Hearle commented. "Such an otherwise clever murderer wouldn't be such a fool."

CHAPTER III

Although he had said that there was little to be done until the next day, Hearle had been speaking figuratively. Critton quickly discovered this, as did the others, for Hearle found work enough that night to occupy the county attorney's office, the sheriff's force and the city police as well. And of them all, Hearle himself was the busiest.

So far, as he readily admitted, he had no clues. He was hopeful, even confident, that some would presently turn up. But in a case like this, he wanted to know something about the murdered man, about his business, where he came from. Hearle remembered Kasmin's sudden uneasiness at the prospect of the lights being flashed off, about his picture being taken. Had he had a premonition of death? If so, he must have known that enemies were upon his trail; have been afraid even then. But he had shrugged it aside as unimportant. Scarcely two minutes later, when the lights went on again, he had been found dead. That was worth consideration.

Hearle, at the moment, studying the man, had been confident that he did not fear the dark, that what he really disliked was having his picture taken. If so, then death had crept up on him unexpectedly. But Hearle might be wrong. Anyway, he found several questions for the others to find the answers to. And by morning he had them.

27

Leadley, questioned concerning Kasmin, said that he really knew little about the man. He had met him on the west coast, had invited him to join the party on the vacation trip. Kasmin claimed to be a retired business man from Indiana. That was really all that Leadley knew about him.

"He may have seen Indiana, since it's not far from Chicago," the sheriff reported, late that night. "But it's a cinch he never lived there while he was in business. I took his finger-prints, like you suggested, and I found them in the records, all right. Seems as if he was one of the biggest racketeers in Chicago until about four months ago. Then things got so hot for him that he had to leave, or be put on the spot—rival gangsters, you know. The police weren't after him."

This had all been confirmed by wires from the Chicago police. Hearle smiled quietly.

"I thought that he looked and acted like a racketeer," he said. "I've dealt with too many of them to be easily fooled, even when they speak reasonably good English and act fairly comfortable in society, as he did. Besides, I thought I'd seen his face in Rogues' Gallery."

Oliver agreed. "He served a sentence several years ago for something."

"Well, that's his past," Hearle nodded. "Which might very well account for his being camera-shy."

"And there's your motive, too, eh?" spoke up Critton. "Some of the other gangsters have been after him, and finally found him here. Just another gangster killing. It lets the others of the party out, considering who he was."

"Maybe," agreed Hearle. "Maybe. Again,

28

maybe not. We really haven't a thing to go on, so far, except guess work."

Morning found Hearle apparently as fresh as ever, though most of the others showed the strain of the night. Having breakfasted, and with Critton by his side, Hearle began the real series of investigations.

First, he called in the night clerk who had been on duty at the time of the murder, but he could report nothing suspicious. A bell-boy, however, who had shown some of the guests up to the suite on arrival, did have something to tell.

"That quiet gentleman with the brown hair, just a touch of gray in it, you know—"

"Mr. Sargent?"

"Yes, that's him, all right. Well, last night, him and this fellow that got bumped off, met outside in the hallway, and I heard them talking. I happened to be going down the hall at the other end, to the elevator, so I couldn't help but hear, though they didn't see me. Looked to me like they'd both just met there. And they were sure mad at each other."

"Mad at each other, eh? How do you know that?"

"By the way they talked, and the language they used. I didn't catch many of the words, for of course I didn't stop to pry. But Mr. Sargent seemed to be doing most of the talking. His voice was low and sort of quiet, but there was a kind of a—a sort of something in it, if you get me, that showed how mad he was. And I did catch the last words he said:

" 'Remember,' he said, 'I've warned you. And

if necessary, I'll kill you like a rattlesnake, and with just as little com——com——' "

"Compunction?"

"That's it. Them was his very words, I remember them clear enough. And Mr. Kasmin stood there, half a head taller and a lot broader, and his face got red, but he didn't say anything more at all. Just turned and moved off down the hall and stared out the window. Sargent waited a minute until a dame, his daughter I guess it was, joined him. Then he went on in."

"That puts a different light on the whole subject," interjected Critton. "Sargent threatening to murder him, and then Kasmin being found dead a little later."

"It's worth bearing in mind." Hearle handed the boy a dollar. "Keep quiet about this," he warned.

"We'll have to ask Sargent about this," Critton declared, briskly.

But inquiries developed the fact that both Leadley and Richard Sargent had driven away early that morning, heading for Leadley's dude ranch on the Dearborn. They had left word that there was some urgent business to attend to, but they would be back that afternoon.

"I don't like the looks of this at all." Critton looked worried. I think we'd better send the sheriff out after them."

"I wouldn't take quite so drastic a step as that, just yet," Hearle cautioned. "Neither of them is foolish enough to try to escape, even if either of them were guilty—and we have no real grounds for supposing that either of them is. No, I think that we will fnd them safely back of their own accord this afternoon. Let's see what else we can turn up in the meantime."

Joan Sargent, fresh and sparkling as the morning after the rain, met them and readily consented to answer any questions that might be asked. Hearle studied her for a moment with puzzled attention. She was not over eighteen, and strikingly beautiful, with the same finely distinguished air of her father. But there was something else about her, as about Richard Sargent himself, that reminded Hearle of something which he yet could not place. It worried him.

"Had you, or your father, known Mr. Kasmin long?" Hearle asked.

"Only a short time," Joan replied. "You see, the whole party has just come here from the coast. And we only became acquainted with Mr. Kasmin on this trip, and that was a very superficial acquaintance. We really knew scarcely anything about him."

"Your father had never known him before, either?"

"Never."

"You're sure of that?"

"Yes, I'm quite positive of it."

"Then I don't suppose that either of you would be able to suggest any possible motive for the—affair, last night, or anything about it?"

"I'm afraid not."

"Did anything about the whole proceedings last night strike you as odd—extraordinary, or anything?"

"Well—I thought that the lights were off a long

31

time. As I understood it, they were to go off for
only two or three seconds. It was an idea of Mr.
Leadley's, to catch everybody sort of off-guard,
as it were."

"Off-guard?"

"Don't misunderstand me, please, Mr. Hearle.
You see, I was there when he was discussing it with
Mr. Pinard, and Mr. Pinard is a famous director.
They both agreed that such a method would result in everybody's appearing more natural—not
posed, if you understand what I mean. And of
course they are strong for anything like that—life-
like pictures."

"Ah yes, I see. And the lights were to be off
for only two or three seconds, then?"

"That was what they said. Merely long enough
to accomplish the purpose of naturalness."

"And something went wrong—due to the murderer himself, I suppose. You didn't detect anything suspicious, otherwise, while the lights were
off?"

"I don't believe that I did."

"You didn't hear anyone get up from his chair,
or move about?"

"I thought that I did, yes. But I have no idea as
to who it was."

"It wasn't Mr. Leadley, on your left, or Mr.
Pinard, on your right?"

"No, I am sure that they both remained seated
all the time."

"You were seated directly opposite Mr. Kasmin.
Didn't you hear anything suspicious?"

"Well, he—he seemed to sigh, once. That was
all, I think."

"When was that?"

"About a minute before the lights went on."

"I judged that the lights were off about two minutes, in all. What would you say?"

"Why, yes, about that, I think, Mr. Hearle. Though it did seem an age, at the time."

"And Mr. Kasmin didn't get up from his chair?"

"I'm quite sure he didn't."

"H'm. You knew, of course, that your father had quarreled seriously with Mr. Kasmin, just before the dinner began?"

A sudden startled widening of the eyes rewarded him for this unexpected shot. Joan gasped, then quickly recovered her composure. Her eyes were suspicious when she answered, her words carefully chosen.

"Why, no, I didn't know it."

"And you have no idea as to why they were quarreling? No idea of the motive?"

"No, how should I have?"

"Ah, how, indeed?" Hearle sighed. He found himself greatly admiring this cool young lady, so loyal to her father, and he saw that he would get nothing more from her. But he was quite convinced that she knew a good deal more than she was telling.

"Well, that will be all now," he said.

"I still think that we should send the sheriff after Sargent," Critton exploded, once the girl had left the room. "They had no business sneaking out that way this morning."

"Sneak, is scarcely the word, Mr. Critton,"
Hearle expostulated mildly. "In fact, they obtained
permission from me to make the trip. Of course, I
had not heard what the bell-boy had to say then,
in regard to Sargent, but even if I had known, I
would probably have granted it."

CHAPTER IV

"I think," decided Hearle, "that we will ask Miss Dixon to sit in the chair of inquisition next. I find her a most interesting personage."

"So do millions of others," retorted Critton. "But I doubt if she will know much about this case."

Hearle's mind was reviewing the events of the evening before—in especial, the talk when it had veered to China, his own tale of the Van Horn murder case. Dolores Dixon had followed the whole conversation with a strained attention that left her face almost white. He remembered, also, that she was said to have traveled widely, which was why she could depict so many varied characterizations so vividly and true to life. Yet that, of course, could have nothing to do with the present murder case of a notorious Chicago racketeer.

Dolores Dixon was fresh and vivacious as ever this morning. Clearly, she was sufficient of an actress to disguise her real feelings, and felt the necessity of "playing up" to her public at all times.

"I suppose that you have all the necessary information all tucked up your sleeve already, clues and all such things, Mr. Hearle?" she greeted.

"You'd be surprised at the dearth of ideas that I have unearthed, to date," Hearle smiled. "Might I ask how long you have known Mr. Kasmin?"

"About three weeks," was the prompt reply. "He

35

came down to the studio one day, with one of the higher-ups of the company piloting him. He claimed to be a retired business man, and he was really very nice. I suppose I am, in a way, responsible for his death here, since I asked Mr. Leadley to invite him on this trip."

"You liked him, then?"

"I did, yes. He seemed so out of place, and yet he was trying, rather pathetically hard, to have a good time. Of course, and I guess I might as well tell you this too, while I'm about it, I didn't fall for him very hard, and I wouldn't have thought of inviting him on my own account. But he had quite a bit of money that he claimed to be interested in investing in the company, and we all had word to treat him nicely and keep him interested. But I did like him."

"Ah, I see. That accounts for his presence, then. I couldn't quite understand that. By the way, had he, do you know, been acquainted with the Sargents prior to this trip?"

"No, I don't think so. In fact, I introduced them, I think."

"I see. And they got on well together?"

"I guess so. They scarcely knew each other, really."

"And did Mr. Kasmin get on well with the other members of the party?"

"He seemed to."

"Did he know any of them before this trip?"

"I don't think so."

"And that brings us down to last night. You were seated next to him, I believe—he was on your left. Did anything strike you as unusual?"

36

Her reactions, however, had been very similar to those of Joan Sargent, and she could add nothing new. She was positive that neither Leadley nor Kasmin had stood up during the period of darkness. Of the others, she could not be sure.

"Have you ever been in China?" Hearle asked suddenly.

For just a moment, Dolores Dixon's face whitened. Then she smiled.

"I may have been," she said calmly. "I traveled a great deal in the charge of others, while I was a small child. Since I was old enough to remember, however, I have not been there."

"You were left an orphan at an early age?"

"Yes."

Hearle tried other questions, apparently aimless, but for some reason or other she was suddenly on her guard, and while willing to talk, she gave no more information.

"We don't seem to be getting anywhere," commented Critton.

"No, we don't," agreed Hearle. "And still, you never can tell. Sometimes a lot of little things when well mixed together and sifted out again, mean a great deal. We will try Mr. Pinard next."

The director, this morning, was dressed in hiking trousers of khaki and polished leather walking boots, topped off by a white shirt loosely opened at the throat, and he seemed much more pleased in these clothes than he had been the night before. Pinard seemed preoccupied, but he was courteously attentive.

As before, Hearle went back to California and events leading up to the night of the murder, but he learned nothing new there. He did, however, uncover one surprising bit of information. Dolores Dixon was Pinard's wife.

"That is news to me," Hearle confessed. "I had never heard that she was married."

"We were married five years ago, when she was sixteen," Pinard explained. "She was scarcely known at all then, as a movie star, of course."

"Oh, I understand. I'd think, Mr. Pinard, that, even knowing her to be your own and faithful, that you would feel a twinge of jealousy now and then, having such a popular wife, loved by so many, courted as an unmarried woman—and so on. I know I would."

Pinard laughed shortly.

"That's all surface froth," he said. "And we get used to it, overlook it. I couldn't afford to be jealous, anyway, since it's my wife's popularity that makes her fortune."

"Of course. Your wife is widely traveled, I believe?"

"Very widely. There's scarcely a corner of the world that she hasn't seen, at some time or other."

"Strange that her publicity agents haven't played that up more."

Pinard's jaws tightened.

"Not so strange," he said. "I knocked one reporter cold for insisting, and since then they have kind of taken the hint. You see," he went on, confidentially, "Dolores was rather a waif, and I gather that she had an unpleasant childhood. In fact she has a positive horror of all remembrances connected with her early youth, and refuses to mention those years, even to me."

Pinard could throw no new light on the murder. Jouralmon was next questioned. He was quite himself today, despite tired lines under his eyes.

"Getting on in years a trifle," he explained. "But I've knocked about so much that it takes a lot to upset me very much."

He, too, had joined the party at Hollywood, and knew Kasmin only superficially.

"Personally," he said, "I was surprised at Leadley's including him in the party. He wasn't our type. But I didn't question Leadley, of course."

"You were seated between the Misses Ferguson, last night?"

"I was. And charming company I found them to be."

"You were on the same side of the table, of course, as Kasmin. Did you hear anything unusual?"

"I didn't, no. Whoever did it was cat-footed, and, I should say, an old hand at such a game. He didn't bungle."

"True enough. And now, as a man of the world, Mr. Jouralmon, have you any suspicions?"

Jouralmon pondered a moment. Finally he nodded.

"I have a bit of information that seems to have escaped you so far," he admitted. "I was reluctant to give it last night, and am still; and I may add that I'm quite sure it's a misleading trail, purposely so. But I'll let yourself and future events be the judge of that.

"I came up to these rooms yesterday forenoon to see Mr. Leadley for a moment, before he went out to his ranch, which he did yesterday afternoon.

Gage met me at the door and asked me to go on in by myself, which I did. As I came into this room, I saw Mr. Leadley and Mr. Sargent seated together on that davenport over there. Mr. Sargent had a long, narrow case, of exquisite design—teakwood, I should say—open on his lap. I had only a glimpse, but I saw that it was filled with what I took to be a very fine, and undoubtedly a very rare, collection of Chinese daggers. I suppose that he collects them as a hobby. In fact, I have heard that he does."

"Chinese daggers!" Critton exclaimed.

"Exactly. He had been showing them to Mr. Leadley, I gathered. I came in rather unexpectedly, of course, and I evidently startled them. Anyway, Mr. Sargent closed his case hastily—he did not know who was coming, I imagine, and naturally he would not display his treasures to every curious eye. But I saw him put back the blade that had just been in Mr. Leadley's hands—and last night, accordingly, I recognized the dagger that was sticking in Mr. Kasmin's back."

For a space there was silence. Hearle drew a slow breath.

"It was the same one?"

"The same one, yes."

Critton leaped to his feet.

"That makes it clear enough," he cried. "One of them—Sargent, probably, did it. And now they're taking this chance to make good their getaway. They'll be over in the next county by now, across the border into Canada in a little while. Where's a phone? I'm going to send the sheriff after them right now."

40

It was Jouralmon who held up a restraining hand.

"If you will pardon me, Mr. Critton, I see no cause for all of this excitement. I would have given this information before, if I had considered that there was any occasion to use it to prevent the escape of a criminal. As I pointed out before, this is most likely a false trail. I would be the last one to accuse either Mr. Sargent or Mr. Leadley of such a crime. The weapon, of course, would have been used by the murderer with the intent of throwing suspicion upon Mr. Sargent. Accordingly, if Sargent was doing such a deed, I do not believe that he would have been so foolish as to use it. It could be traced back to him too easily.

"Since he was gone during the afternoon," Jouralmon continued, "it would not, I fancy, have been a difficult matter for some one to attain access to his room and to his dagger case. No, I would not be too ready to suspect him."

Critton paused.

"That's so," he admitted. "Still, it's something that has to be considered."

"Surely," agreed Hearle. "And I will consider it in due course. But I still think that both gentlemen will return this afternoon."

Grumbling doubtfully, Critton sank into a chair again.

"Sargent, also, was seated on the opposite side of the table, at the opposite end, from Kasmin," Jouralmon added. "Which would have made it difficult for him to commit the crime."

Hearle made no comment. He was reflecting that Sargent had threatened to kill Kasmin; also, it had been testified that practically every other member of the party had remained seated while the darkness held. Sargent, however, if Hearle's own observations had been accurate, had not only stood up, but he had left his chair, and moved around. He had been directly on Hearle's left.

CHAPTER V

Next on Hearle's list were the daughters of Senator Ferguson. They came in together, frankly ready to help if they could do so. Elinor had been seated on Hearle's right at the table, with Jouralmon on her right, then Margaret, and next, Kasmin himself. But Margaret, while admitting that she heard suspicious sounds, had not been able to place them definitely. Both girls were positive that Jouralmon had not moved from the table during the period of darkness, though they had heard someone moving about.

Critton was disappointed, but Hearle had expected nothing else. One thing was established, however. Every man at the table had kept to his seat, as instructed—except Sargent. Why should Sargent move about, against the request that he remain seated? Perhaps he had some good reason. And what good reason could he have had, other than the wielding of the dagger?

Moreover, the fact remained that he had been back in his chair when the lights did go on again. To move about, against a request, and with the momentary expectation that the lights would flash on and discover him to be doing so, might result in embarassment. Did he have a way of knowing how long the lights would be off, and the proper time to resume his seat?

There remained, of the guests, only Mrs. Reid,

until Leadley and Sargent should return. Mrs. Reid seemed curiously shaken today, as well she might, Hearle reflected.

"I suppose you're thinking all sorts of dreadful things about me," she began at once, tension quivering in her voice. "I talked to you of murders, declared I hoped there would be one, said I felt there would—you must believe that I knew all about it, or even think that I did it."

"No, no, Mrs. Reid, not so bad as that, surely," Hearle replied soothingly. "Tell me just one thing now, on that subject, and then we'll forget it. Did you know, or have reason to suspect anything, in advance?"

"No, I didn't, honestly. Not a thing. I—I was just talking, as usual. I'm a great hand to talk, you know."

"So I had gathered," Hearle agreed bluntly. "But you tried to tell me that you were psychic. Anything to that?"

"Well, I—I felt some sort of a—like an electrical undercurrent in the room, really. It made me rather nervous and excited, though I couldn't explain it, and didn't know how to interpret it. But I really did have a feeling that something was going to happen."

"So did I," Hearle nodded unexpectedly. "Well, putting all that out of our minds, what did you know about Mr. Kasmin before that happened?"

"Very little. In fact, next to nothing, I'm afraid. You know, I suppose, that I came west with Senator Ferguson's daughters, as sort of a chaperon, not that they need one—rather a traveling companion, I suppose, since the Senator

44

couldn't come with them. I met Mr. Kasmin later on, in Hollywood. But—well, we were scarcely on speaking terms, if you understand me."

"I see. You have no idea as to who could have killed him, or a possible motive?"

"No idea at all, I'm sure."

"Mr. Pinard was seated on your left. Did he remain in his chair all during the period of darkness?"

"I'm quite sure that he did."

"And Mr. Sargent, on your right?"

"I did think—of course, it was so dark that I can't be sure—but it did seem to me as though he left his chair for a moment or so."

"Just a moment or so?"

"Well, I don't know. That was all guesswork on my part, anyhow. It may have been longer."

"Did he seem to move around much?"

"I did think that I heard someone moving around."

"And Mr. Jouralmon, who was seated across the table from you? Did he remain seated?"

"Yes, he was in his chair all the time. I know, because his feet kept sort of twitching, or shuffling about on the floor, all the time the lights were out, as though the darkness made him nervous. And once he kicked me."

"Kicked you?"

"Well, I don't suppose that he intended to, of course. He was so nervous that his foot kind of kicked out—just as though he couldn't help himself, you know. And it caught me on the ankle. I had a hard time to keep from screaming."

"Indeed. He must have been nervous. Then it

was his feet that made that little shuffling noise on the floor?"

"Well, they did make a little noise."

"Did you observe as to how well Mr. Kasmin got on with the other members of the party?"

"Why—well enough, I think. I never knew of anything that wasn't as it should be."

Mary Yee repeated what she had said before— that she had been in the room where the ladies had removed their wraps, busy with her work there. Hearle leaned forward intently.

"You naturally had the lights on in there, of course. Tell me: did they go off at the time that they were turned off in the dining room, or not?"

"Why, yes, they did. I thought it rather strange, but I knew they wanted it dark for taking the picture, so I supposed that it had been arranged for all the lights in the suite to go off at the same time."

"That is a point worth remembering," Hearle reflected. "And now tell me, how long have you been in the employ of Miss Dixon?"

"Oh, for many years. About six, I think."

"Ah. Then you were with her before she married Mr. Pinard?"

"Oh yes, before she ever knew him. She was just starting in as an actress."

"Then you can tell me, perhaps, if she and Mr. Pinard are happily married? So many Hollywood couples, I understand, are hardly to be so described."

But on this point Mary Yee had no hesitancy. There was no more happily married couple anywhere, she insisted, either in or out of Hollywood. They adored each other.

"But she received the attentions of many other men?"

"But that is only natural, in her position. Sometimes it is a matter of business, sometimes popularity, sometimes because she likes them. It means nothing, of course."

"Then her husband is never jealous?"

"Not often."

"But he is sometimes?"

"Well, he was awfully jealous of Mr. —" she clapped a hand over her mouth, a frightened look shot into her eyes. "You fool me, I talk too much," she cried.

"You were about to say Mr. Kasmin. Why was he jealous of him?"

Mary Yee stared at him for a moment, trouble in her large eyes. Then she shook her head doubtfully.

"I should not tell you, and anyway, he is the finest man, just as she is a fine woman. It means nothing, really."

"But he was jealous of Mr. Kasmin. Insanely jealous. Why?"

"I think because she went out with Mr. Kasmin several times, and Mr. Pinard did not like Mr. Kasmin. You see—well, with men like Mr. Leadley, he knows that with them, it is only a business, and it means not much. Or men of that type—they are gentlemen. But with Mr. Kasmin—well, I do not think that Mr. Kasmin knew that she was married at all, you see. And of course she did not tell him. Then, Mr. Kas-

47

min was a different sort—not a gentleman, if you understand."

"I understand. And I can scarcely blame Mr. Pinard."

"But you were on the trip—you knew, too," Mary Yee charged.

"You forget," Hearle pointed out, "that I met only a few members of the party one day in Hollywood, and then had other business, so that I did not rejoin the party until yesterday afternoon, here in Helena."

"Oh yes, I had forgotten, Mr. Hearle. Pardon me."

"Of course. Can you tell me what Mr. Pinard and Mr. Sargent were doing yesterday forenoon?"

"Yes. They both slept late, as we had been late in arriving the night before—the train was late. After a tardy breakfast, both of them went out with Mr. Leadley in his car. I heard them say that they were going to ride around town a little. It was after eleven o'clock when the three of them came back together, and went into a sitting room. Mr. Sargent was telling them that he was going to show them something. After a few minutes, Mr. Jouralmon also arrived and went in, and then all four of them came out after a little and went to lunch."

Hearle blinked. So Pinard had been in thère too, looking at the daggers! Jouralmon had carefully refrained from any mention of this. Pinard likewise must have recognized that dagger that had killed Kasmin—but he had not seen fit to mention it today. Also, Pinard had been furiously jealous of his wife, angry at Kasmin. And yet—Joan Sargent and Mrs. Reid had been certain that Pinard had remained seated all during the period of darkness.

"Was Kasmin at all intimate with any other members of the party?"

"Oh, Mr. Leadley was always very nice to him. And then there was Mrs. Reid."

"She was on—er, more than speaking terms with him, then?"

"I would think so, yes. They were out to various dinners, parties, shows—you know, together, in Hollywood, though they only had a couple of days there. On the train they saw little of each other, but when they could be alone— well, I gathered that they must be old acquaintances. I supposed that they were old friends; had known each other for some time."

"I see. And they were the only ones that Mr. Kasmin was at all intimate with?"

"Well, he tried to be with Miss Sargent. She would hardly look at him, of course, but he seemed to think that he was a great ladies' man. I think that Mr. Sargent had to warn him two or three times that he was not to bother her, but I don't know as it did much good."

"You seem to be very observant, Miss Yee."

"It is my business, in a way, sir."

"Anything else—anyone else, that he bothered?"

Mary Yee colored slightly.

"No one else, I guess—unless it might be me. He tried to kiss me a couple of times."

"Indeed? I see what you mean by 'ladies' man'."

"Yes, he was that way, I guess. He didn't

bother the Misses Ferguson much, I guess, but they kept pretty well to themselves, and always together. So maybe that was because of lack of opportunity."

"Which would account for it. By the way, did Mr. Leadley ever have occasion to warn Mr. Kasmin, do you think?"

"No, I don't think so, sir. Mr. Leadley is a fine young man, but then, he's rather blind at times—especially of late."

"Why of late, especially?"

"Chiefly, I think, because he has—in a way of speaking, at least—known Miss Joan Sargent only recently. But he seems to be far gone—which is an unusual thing with him, sir. He smiles at every woman and is nice to them, but he's one of the few very eligible young men in Hollywood who haven't had any affairs of any sort."

"And so he's interested in Joan Sargent, eh?" muttered Hearle, to himself. "And today he has gone off with Richard Sargent. Hum."

CHAPTER VI

Hearle glanced expectantly at Critton. But for once the prosecutor had nothing to say. Instead, he threw up his hands expressively and shook his head.

"I'm sunk," he confessed. "The deeper you dig, the more confusing it becomes. What next?"

"Next will be Gage, I think," Hearle decided. "We haven't heard his story, yet. It's really astounding," he added, "that several people can be all together in a room, most of them seated about a dinner table, and when something happens, know so little about it—and have such widely varied reactions."

"That's the devil of a prosecutor's job," Critton agreed. "What would I do with that bunch on the witness stand, at the present stage of proceedings? Absolutely nothing. And yet they're a fair sample. It's in your hands, Hearle."

Gage appeared. He was the perfect gentleman's gentleman, as ever, and he sat down very carefully in a chair when asked to, still very much at attention.

"I want you to tell me just what happened to you last night, Gage," Hearle requested. "In the first place, how long were the lights supposed to be off?"

"Not above two or three seconds, sir. Just long

enough to fool the guests into thinking that it would last longer, so that they wouldn't be posing at all. A little hobby of Mr. Leadley's, sir."

"All right. Tell it in your own way."

"Well, as you know, sir, I had the camera all set up on the tripod, and everything ready. Just behind me a step was the light switch, and I reached back, without even looking, because I knew just where it was, and turned the lights out. Almost at once then, I pressed the button which started the camera to operating, since it was already focused properly. It ran automatically, you see, once it was turned on. All of that took only a couple of seconds.

"After that, believing everything to be ready, I prepared to turn the lights on again. I reached back and pressed the button, and it pushed in all right—there was no catch or anything like that, which might have caused the trouble. But the lights didn't go on.

"Naturally, sir, I was puzzled. I wondered if I had somehow made a mistake, so I pushed both buttons on and off two or three times with my fingers, just to make sure. But it didn't make any difference. So, as I had had the forethought to place a small flash-light there on the little stand beside me, I felt for it, intending to flash it on to reassure the guests, and to use it to find out what was wrong. I felt carefully over the whole table top for it, but it was gone!

"It was then that Mr. Leadley asked me what was the trouble. I was beginning to realize that something was seriously wrong, but not wishing to alarm the guests and perhaps create a panic there in the darkness, I merely replied that the lights wouldn't seem to go on again, but that I would get them in a moment. Perhaps, considering what subsequently happened, I did wrong, but at the time I did not realize that there could be anything gravely amiss. Mr. Leadley told me to use my flash-light, and I agreed. I thought that perhaps it had fallen off the table on to the floor, and that I would find it at the foot of the stand.

"So I got down on my hands and knees and began fumbling around, in an effort to find it. But I couldn't. In fact, Mr. Hearle, that flash-light had completely disappeared, and I haven't seen it since.

"While I was kneeling on the floor," he went on carefully, "something fell from somewhere, a tiny object. I heard it hit the floor, with a faint noise, sort of a ping! It bounded a little when it hit, and struck my hand. My fingers closed on it, and I put it in my pocket. I had completely forgotten it until just now, with all the ensuing excitement, you know, sir. Trying to remember what happened, I just now recalled it. Here it is, sir."

Gage fumbled in his coat pocket a moment, brought out a small round object—a small white button, like a shirt button. He handed this to Hearle.

"Whoever lost it," commented Hearle, "must have been exercising violently just then—contorting himself, or something, as a man would in driving a dagger deep into the heart of another. In other words, it is highly probable that here we

53

have a button from off the murderer's shirt, Gage."

Gage appeared startled.

"That may very likely be so, sir."

"I wish that you had remembered it last night," Hearle went on. "The omission will doubtless have been repaired by now, once its owner discovered his loss. Still, I did not notice any shirt button or otherwise missing, did you, Gage?"

"None, sir. As a matter of fact, every gentleman was dressed in evening dress, and none of the shirts worn could have contained buttons like that, sir."

"Quite true. None of the clothing worn by anyone could have had that button on, eh?"

"Well, sir, I would scarcely go so far as to say that. It is possible. Again, it could have been off of some article of underclothing."

"In other words, we have a very important clue that is apt to be impossible to trace. But keep your eyes open, Gage, as you go about your work."

"I will, sir, indeed. Well, to resume. Being unable to find the flash-light, I stood up again— and as I did so, the lights flashed on again. I had apparently left the switch on."

"And how do you account for all of that, Gage?"

"Well, sir, though the shades were drawn at the time, I noticed that the lights of the street did not go out, and I heard you inquire of the clerk if the lights were affected in the rest of the hotel. Since they were not, there can be only one explanation. In a little room off the hall, outside, is a switch for turning the current of the whole suite on or off. Someone must have known that I was going to turn the lights off. In that case, he would probably know that the lights would be off for only a second or so. So he must have been at that little room, ready, and the instant that I turned the lights off, he pulled the switch, so that they would not go back on again."

"But why should he wait for you to turn the lights off?" interposed Critton. "If it is as you say, he could have pulled the switch and plunged the room into darkness at any time."

"Yes sir, so he could, sir," agreed Gage. "I thought of that. But to have done so at any other moment would, of course, have alarmed the guests. By taking the moment when he did, the guests would expect the lights to go off, and would not be alarmed, at least for a little while. And he did not require a great deal of time in which to work. As soon as he had finished his job, he turned the switch on again, of course."

"But why should he bother to do that?" Critton demanded. "If he could get around sufficiently well in the dark to murder a man, then he could get away better by leaving the lights off. It would have been that much longer before what had happened was discovered."

"He might have preferred to cast suspicion on some one in the room—myself, for instance," Gage pointed out. "The other way, it would have been shown more clearly to be the work of an outsider."

"That's the only theory that could work," Hearle agreed. "Which leads us to new assumptions, Gage. For no one in the room could possibly have got out and to that switch, and have turned it off, all in a second or so. Even if he could have done so, he couldn't have turned it on later and have been in his seat at the same moment as the lights flashed on, since you left the switch on. Naturally, the lights went on in the room at the same moment as the switch in the hall was turned. Of course, whoever is guilty could have had a confederate, one working inside and one outside of the room."

"Exactly, sir."

"Whoever did it, would have had to be familiar with the room, and with the seating arrangement in use at the moment, as well. Very familiar. The absence of any usual noise, any false movement which would have caused an alarm, proves that."

"Very true, sir, indeed."

"And even then, I don't see how they did it. But the fact remains that it was done. H'm. That closet, or room that the switch is in, would be kept locked, I should think."

"So it would seem, sir. I recalled it a little while ago, sir, and tried it to see. It was not locked. I didn't touch anything, just looked. There might be finger-prints, of course, although I doubt it."

"Small chance, seeing how clever the fellow was with the dagger," Hearle grunted. "But we'll have the sheriff give it the once-over."

"I have taken the liberty, sir," Gage went on, "of having the film sent out to be developed. It was running, you see, sir, when the lights flashed on again, and I didn't think of the machine, to stop it, for quite ten minutes afterward. It occurred to me that the eye of the camera might have detected something which the rest of us failed to see. The

56

film should be back very soon now."

"Gage, you're perfect," Hearle approved. "Did any of the guests move about, do you think? While it was dark, I remember that you asked them to please remain quiet."

"I think that one of them did, sir. Mr. Sargent, I believe. But why, I could do no more than guess."

"And your guess?"

"I'd hate to guess, sir, since it doesn't seem to fit."

"That's the way I feel about guessing," Hearle sighed. "Call up Mr. Oliver, Critton, and have him get busy on that switch. And ask them downstairs about how it happens to be unlocked. I'll question Jouralmon's boy, Yamamoto, and then we've gone over the list, except for Sargent's story, and Leadley's."

Yamamoto, Hearle found to be a yellow man of about thirty-five or so, tall and lank, yet with a rather wizened face none the less, so that at second glance he might as easily have passed for fifty. His was an expressionless face, despite a perpetual smile which revealed glistening teeth. His English was reasonably good, and he seemed willing to talk.

"I work for Mr. Jouralmon for many, many years, yes," he agreed. "He pick me up in Philippines, I not much more than boy then. Treat me good. I work for him steady, ever since. We travel a lot. India, Africa, England, Panama, Alaska, New York, yes, lot all time everywhere.

"Last night, I in Mr. Jouralmon's room, down on floor below, unpack trunks, suit case, tend to my duties for oh, long time. I not come up to Mr.

Leadley's suite at all until I called to tell where I been. I not know anything about what been happening till then. I answer your question, then I go straight back down again, finish work."

Despite further questioning, he added nothing new. Sheriff Oliver strolled in to report disgustedly that the light switch in the hall off the suite had been wiped clean of all finger-prints, and might, or might not, have been used recently. The little room was always kept locked, they reported downstairs. How it could have been open they couldn't understand. But so it was.

Gage appeared, bearing a small package under his arm.

"The film is here," he reported. "I have fixed everything in readiness in another room, if you would care to view it now."

CHAPTER VII

"If you could arrange to stop the film as soon as the lights flash on," suggested Hearle. "So that we could study it carefully."

"Certainly, sir," agreed Gage. "Or I can run it in slow motion, if you like. Mr. Leadley was careful to have the best of equipment in every respect. The lights, although you may not have noticed it, were special lights, to insure a perfect picture."

"Slow motion will be fine," agreed Hearle. "But please stop it for a moment at the start, as well."

Gage started the machine. For nearly two minutes by Hearle's watch, there was only a blank screen, during which time the camera had been running while the lights were off. Then, with startling abruptness, the picture flashed on, and there was the same scene at which Hearle had stared only a few hours before. Almost instantly, Gage stopped the machine, leaving the figures immobile.

Kasmin was there, slumped forward in his chair, the coffee spilling out of his overturned cup. The camera had not been set at the proper angle, however, to reveal the dagger which protruded from his back.

Both Margaret Ferguson and Dolores Dixon were staring at him as the lights went on, wonder in their eyes. As Hearle signaled and the film began

59

to slowly move again, that wonder changed to stark horror.

Every person about the table had been seated in his proper place when the lights went on. Leadley had been staring straight at Kasmin, a slightly puzzled look in his eyes which changed to horror as he saw that his guest was dead. Joan Sargent too, had been looking straight across the table, as though expecting something unusual.

Jouralmon had been staring straight before him when the lights flashed on. Startled incredulity had flashed over his face, followed swiftly by horror and consternation as he turned to look at the man only one chair removed from him. He had grasped the edge of the table as though to steady himself. A moment only had this play of emotion mastered him, however. Then his face was again its usual well-bred mask.

Elinor Ferguson, of the whole company, appeared to have had no inkling beforehand that anything might be wrong in the room. Her emotions were those of one who first discovered from the faces of her neighbors that something was amiss, and who turned then to discover that tragedy had been an unbidden guest at the feast where frivolity was supposed to dominate.

The face of Pinard was cold. Brief surprise had been in his look, a touch of natural horror, but these were very light. It was as if he was scarcely startled at whatever might have happened, and, seeing who the victim was, not particularly ill-pleased.

Mrs. Reid, as Hearle had noted at the time, had displayed the most instant emotion. Her eyes had

flashed instantly to Kasmin, stark terror had leaped
to them, and she had half-risen from her chair, one
hand clapped over her mouth as if to repress a
scream.

Richard Sargent had been, perhaps, the most perfectly self-controlled person at the table, with the
exception of Hearle himself. His eyes had turned
naturally to the focus of attention, his lips had
tightened, eyes half-closed for a moment while he
studied the dead man, curiously, as one not unused
to such scenes, and taking a purely academic interest in the exhibit. One hand, Hearle noted now,
had held a napkin. Now Sargent carefully folded
it and laid it on the table beside his plate, before
pushing back his chair and rising.

"He's altogether too calm," came the voice of
Critton, beside Hearle. "Just as though he knew
beforehand what to expect; that it would be that
way."

The same thought had flashed through Hearle's
mind, with another one equally unpleasant. That
napkin, folded at first into a close ball in Sargent's
fist—a very natural article to use in wiping finger-
prints off the dagger, even off the light-switch in
the little closet outside the hall.

Yet there was something missing in the picture,
assuming that Sargent should be guilty. It would
have been a physical impossibility for him to leave
his chair, go almost the length of the room to the
door, out into the hall, down to the closet, and
pull the switch which threw all the lights off, in
the two or three seconds before Gage pressed the
button again. Or, having committed the murder,
to turn the light switch and be instantly in his

61

seat again. In fact, no one in the room, with the possible exception of Gage himself, could have done it.

Gage might have done it all, without touching the switch out in the hall at all! That was a possibility which could not be overlooked. Though if Gage wished to do it, why should he have moved his camera to the opposite end of the table and the corner opposite Kasmin? He had tried it there at first, then had decided on the other end of the room, as giving the best view.

That was logical, of course, from the point of getting the best picture. For at the other end of the table were both Leadley and Dolores Dixon, and to take it from behind them and at their left would necessitate that they turn in their chairs, and even then, the view would be poor. Such famous stars were accustomed to being in the spotlight in every picture.

By going to the spot where the picture had been taken, there had been only Eric Hearle at the end— one person instead of two. A better view from every standpoint.

It made it more difficult to commit the murder, however, if Gage had done it. Still, it would have been simple enough, and his moving the camera to the opposite end might have been something in the nature of an alibi. Also, that brought him close to the light switch.

However, if lights outside of the room were affected, then one thing was certain. If anyone in the room had committed the crime, he had had a confederate outside, to turn the switch at the proper moment. Or it might have been someone outside who had done it all.

During lunch, Hearle was abstracted and silent, Critton little less so, though the latter was plainly impatient, nervous at the thought that Sargent might be making his escape with nothing done to hinder him.

This impatience grew on him as the afternoon wore on and the two did not return. The day had grown cloudy again, with the promise of another rainy night. The atmosphere was one of gloom. The towering hills which surrounded the city on every side seemed almost to be closing in, like intangible forebodings of evil. Even Hearle was oppressed by the atmosphere, forced to shake himself roughly to clear his mind.

At mid-afternoon, Critton was restrained from dispatching the sheriff only by calling up the ranch on the Dearborn and discovering that both men had arrived there on schedule, had remained somewhat longer than they had planned on, Leadley being very busy, but were now on the way back to Helena.

Night had finally settled when they returned. At word of their arrival, Critton, who had gone to his office, hurried back, and Leadley, on Hearle's request, came in to tell what he knew.

"Mr. Sargent went right up to his rooms," he explained. "He wanted to freshen up a bit for dinner."

"Sorry to have to make such a nuisance of ourselves, Leadley," Hearle smiled. "I'm afraid you'll never invite me to a party of yours again."

"I surely will, though," Leadley retorted vigorously. "I'm very much interested in having you get to the bottom of this affair. It has upset me rather badly. I suppose I shouldn't have chased off to the ranch today, but there have been some things piling up there, for me to attend to, and they simply had to be looked after."

Leadley was able to tell nothing new concerning Kasmin, up to the night before. Hearle abruptly shifted to the subject of the daggers.

"Did you recognize the weapon that killed Mr. Kasmin last night?" he demanded.

"Why, no, I can't say that I did," Leadley replied uncertainly.

"Didn't Mr. Sargent show you that same weapon, along with several others—you and Mr. Pinard —yesterday forenoon?"

"Well, he showed us a lot of daggers of his collection, certainly," Leadley admitted. "Over a dozen of them, I guess. And that one might have been among them. I don't know. I'll confess that I wondered a bit when I saw it in—last night, but so many of them looked so much alike to me, that I couldn't say for sure whether it was one of Sargent's or not."

"And that was why you didn't mention it before?"

"Naturally. I didn't care to go casting suspicion where I had only guesswork to go on."

"Um. As you know, Leadley, I was with you a couple of days in Hollywood, but I met only a few members of this present party while I was there. Then I traveled here alone, having other business. So I never met the Sargents until yesterday. How long have you known them, what do you know about them, and how do they happen to be in this party?"

"I've known them for several years—six or eight, at least. So, when I happened to discover them down in Hollywood not so long ago, and since I was making up a little party of friends to come up here and spend my vacation with me, I naturally asked them along." Leadley paused, actually flushed.

"I hadn't seen Joan Sargent for about four years, until recently," he added. "I might confess to you, gentlemen, that she was one reason for my asking them; though I greatly esteem Mr. Sargent himself as a friend."

"Your reasons appear to be excellent ones," Hearle smiled. "But you haven't fully answered my question as to what you know about them?"

"I know Mr. Sargent to be just what he appears to be—a gentleman, in the fullest sense of the word. I don't know that I can say more than that. Why?" he shot out suddenly. "You surely don't suspect him in this case? That would be ridiculous!"

"It may be ridiculous," Critton snapped, "but, unless he can give some very good explanation for his actions, we're going to find it necessary to place him under arrest."

Leadley turned and regarded the prosecutor in some amazement.

"Arrest Sargent?" he repeated. "You must be crazy. He's as mild and peaceful a man as you will find the wide world over."

"Those are just the sort who are most dangerous when aroused," Critton retorted.

"But it's unthinkable, in the case of Sargent. What possible motive could he have?"

"His motive appears to have been Kasmin's attentions to his daughter. Just before your dinner last night, Sargent threatened to kill Kasmin."

"I don't believe it," Leadley growled. "It's all tommy-rot—a put-up job somewhere." He turned to Hearle. "You surely don't believe any such thing as that, do you?"

"It doesn't look reasonable to me," Hearle confessed. "None the less, there are certain grave factors which are unexplained. He will be given an opportunity to tell what he knows, and perhaps he can satisfy us on those points. If not—well, I'm afraid my young friend here will insist on his arrest."

"You're right, I will," Critton agreed. "Shall we go and see him now?"

"Shortly," nodded Hearle. "There are one or two more questions that I want to ask you first, Leadley. Whose idea was it that the lights should be turned off in the first place, last night? Don't say that it was your idea unless you're quite sure that it was. Did somebody else suggest it to you in the first place?"

Leadley reflected a moment, nodded.

"It was Pinard's idea," he said. "He is a great director, as you know, and he knows just how to handle such things."

"How long were the lights to be off?"

"About two or three seconds."

Outside now, the night had grown black, with rain beating steadily against the windows, rattling in small gusts very similar to the evening before.

With its coming, the evening had grown chilly. Leadley stood up, his face thoughtful, almost sulky; moved to a small, hidden clothes-closet, took out from it the same dinner coat that he had worn the evening before, which Hearle remembered he had taken off and thrown across a chair, when, in shirt-sleeves, he had assisted the officers with the body. Now, with a characteristically careless disregard of whether it was the proper thing or not, he slipped it on again.

Hearle smiled slightly to himself at the naturalness of this action; leaned forward.

"What's that in your pocket?" he asked.

Leadley thrust a hand in readily enough, drew out a small flashlight, and stared at it in amazement.

"How does this come to be here, in my pocket? It's my flash-light—the same one that Gage was using last night."

"I thought it looked like it," Hearle agreed.

"But how on earth did it come to be in my pocket?" Leadley repeated.

"That's what we'd like to know, too," Critton commented drily. "How?"

Leadley stared at him, and seemed for the first time to realize the significance of the thing.

"But it was over on this stand, the last I saw of it. You don't think I could have done all that, do you?"

"Since those who sat on either side of you are positive that you didn't leave your chair, it seems unlikely that you could have walked to the other end of the room and back," Hearle said. 'It looks as though whoever took it, did it to keep Gage from using it, then slipped it in your pocket to get rid of it."

"This whole thing is getting to be darned queer," said Leadley.

"Let's go and see Sargent now," Critton insisted.

Together, the three walked down the hall to Sargent's rooms at the opposite side, knocked, but receiving no response, walked in. Leadley had said that Sargent had come straight to his rooms only a little while ago, to dress for dinner. But now his rooms were empty.

A swift search of the hotel, inquiries, revealed the fact that no one had seen Richard Sargent since he had left Leadley. He had disappeared.

CHAPTER VIII

Shortly after the disappearance of Richard Sargent was discovered, the rain stopped, but activity about the hotel and city continued feverishly. Critton was positive now that Sargent had been unnerved and made an effort at escape. As the hours dragged and no trace of him was found, he became furious. A little of this rage he vented on Eric Hearle himself.

"You had no business to let him go in the first place, this morning," he charged. "And if you hadn't delayed me for so long, I'd have had him arrested long ago, before he had a chance to run. The case was clear enough all along. I'm almost inclined to think that you've been purposely protecting him. In fact, how do we know that you aren't mixed up in the whole thing yourself? You were there, and though everybody else has been questioned, you haven't. I'm almost inclined—"

"What?" demanded Hearle, as he paused. "You're almost inclined to do what?"

"As an officer of the law, I'm almost inclined to have you arrested as an accomplice."

Hearle smiled slightly, patiently. Slowly he delved into a pocket, drew out a small leather case, extracted from it a document and passed it over to Critton. The latter, as he read it, flushed red. At the conclusion he was for a moment speechless.

69

"I—I guess this has got on my nerves, and I let my tongue run away with me," he stammered. "I apologize."

"I understand," agreed Hearle. "But I trust that, as a special Federal officer and licensed detective, that you no longer question my authority or my good intentions to conduct this case as I may see fit?"

"Certainly not," Critton agreed. "I had rather imagined that I was in charge of this case, but I see that your authority supersedes mine."

"I do not wish to have to use my authority as a Federal officer, in this," Hearle explained. "I hold it merely for emergencies. This case will continue to be in the hands of the county authorities, and I will work with you as a private investigator."

Nothing appeared to have been disturbed in Sargent's rooms. If he had tried to escape, then he had taken nothing with him. Joan Sargent, though she preserved an outward calm under this latest shock, was torn by anxiety. She had not seen her father since his return, she said.

"But he would never run away, no matter what might be against him." She defended her father proudly. "He would stay and face it. He is no coward."

"If you would tell us just what you know," Hearle suggested, "it might be of help in finding him. If he didn't run away, then that is all the more reason why we should find him. Evidence, you know," he added gently, "may sound very damning in the ears of one who knows only one side of a case. That same evidence, making part of a whole, may fit in in an entirely different way."

"Oh, I believe you're right," the girl sighed. "I can't understand this—why he should disappear. But whatever his reason, it will be a good one, believe me, or he would not do it. And I do feel that you are honest, kind—that you aren't the sort to judge one little fact off by itself, and make it seem terrible."

"I trust not. I have long ago learned that that is the surest way to go wrong."

"Tell him whatever you may know, Joan," urged Elinor Ferguson, putting her arm protectingly about the other girl's shoulders. Joan and the Ferguson girls, Hearle noted approvingly, were already warm friends, though they had known each other only a few days.

"I'm going to admit, then, what I suppose you know already," Joan decided. "You asked me before if father and Mr. Kasmin were acquainted, or —or anything. They hadn't been; only a short time; on this trip. Mr. Kasmin did try to annoy me with his attentions, however, and though I didn't say anything to father, he noticed it. And he did warn Mr. Kasmin not to bother me."

"You asked me," she proceeded rather breathlessly, "if they had quarreled before—last night. I didn't know of it, but they may have done so. Father had told me that he was going to give Kasmin a warning that he would understand, so that he wouldn't bother me again. But I know—oh, I know—that father never killed him."

"You take her to bed with you, Elinor," Hearle advised. "She needs you and Margaret to look after her tonight. And what we all need is a little sleep. It has been rather a hard twenty-four

71

hours. As for me, I've interviewed about every-body around here, I guess, including nearly all the hotel employees and a few assorted guests on this floor, none of whom know anything. I'm going to sleep and let a new day help to solve things."

He sought his own room, noted abstractedly that the rain had stopped, though the clouds continued to lower blackly. A wind that had been about the city earlier in the evening had died away, leav-ing a breathless calm. The noises of the street be-low were becoming hushed at this hour. A railroad engine whistled somewhere, then slumber claimed Eric Hearle.

Brilliant sunshine was streaming into his room when he awoke. It was a glorious spring day. Hearle knew a poignant moment of regret, as he leaned out of his window and breathed the brac-ing air of the Rockies, fresh washed from the rain, that this affair should have intruded. He would greatly have preferred to go on to Leadley's big ranch in the mountains, as had been planned, to re-lax, whip the streams for trout, enjoy a vacation. He smiled wryly. This promised to be anything but a vacation.

Leadley had insisted that all of his guests should gather, not in the fatal dining room of two days before, but in another room, to breakfast together. But a strained air still gripped everyone. For no trace of Richard Sargent had been found during the night. In the middle of the meal, however, the phone rang, and Critton's voice called Hearle to answer.

"I've just discovered that a private plane left the airport not long after Leadley and Sargent returned last evening," he reported. "It hasn't returned, or been heard of since. I'm afraid that it must have headed for Canada with him on board. If it did, of course he's safely across the line a long time ago."

"Thanks for keeping me posted," Hearle answered, and went back to his breakfast. Joan Sargent's face seemed to lighten a little when he told what the message had been. Hearle ate abstractedly. Why should Sargent choose to go off that way, without telling anyone? He must have a very good reason for it, since it made the case against him appear ten times blacker than it had before. Always supposing, of course, that he really was a passenger in the mystery plane.

But breakfast was scarcely finished when a car stopped outside the hotel, and a few minutes later, Sheriff Oliver rushed into the room.

"I'd like for you to come with me, Mr. Hearle. If you can spare the time right now."

His voice was almost determinedly careless, his gaze was bent studiously on the floor, his voice hushed, while he twisted his hat nervously in his hands. Joan Sargent, her own face white, pushed her way forward, paused before him.

"What is it, sheriff?" she demanded. "Have you found my father? Tell me."

Oliver reddened uncomfortably, looked about as though for a way of escape.

"I—I'm not sure," he stammered. "I hope not."

"You hope not?" There was a catch in her voice. "But you think that you have," Joan cried. "Tell me, please, just what you know. I have the right to know."

The sheriff looked about the room. Clearly he did not relish this task, but there was no escape for him. Joan's eyes were searching his face, while she waited for the answer.

"A man has been found, down in what is called the jungle, beyond the railroad tracks," Oliver finally confessed. "A tramp found him there a little while ago. I—it probably isn't your father, Miss Sargent. But we were just going to town to see if it had any bearing on this case."

Joan Sargent went deathly white for an instant, then reeled. Leadley sprang forward and caught her, his face nearly as white as her own. Despite his words, it was easy to see what the sheriff really feared. But after a moment Joan smiled slightly at him, and straightened.

"I'm all right, thank you. You—from the description, did you think—" her voice broke, went on bravely. "But I know you did. I am going, also."

"Oh, I wouldn't, if I were you—" the sheriff shrugged, glanced about at the others for help. But Joan was determined. A moment later, accompanied by Hearle and Leadley, they descended to the car, where Critton was already waiting. Another police car had preceded them.

They drove swiftly, coming in a few minutes to the section, largely overgrown with weeds and willows, called the "jungle" where passing tramps were accustomed to stop. Many little paths ran here and there in the high grass, like rabbit trails, a few rude ovens and shelters had been constructed, and junk of many sorts, gathered by the wayfarers and left for their successors, was strewn about. The brush and grass still gleamed wetly, as with dew, from the rain of the night before, and everything was muddy. Not far away, though almost invisible, a switching engine puffed importantly with many little false starts and pauses.

"A tramp reported it this morning," Critton explained to Hearle, low-toned. "He came in, pretty badly frightened, to the police station, and said that he had been going along a path down here and almost stepped on a dead man lying there. He was careful not to disturb anything, he said, but backed away, then came uptown and reported it. The police went down at once, of course, but I heard of it and gave strict orders that they were to keep away and not disturb things until we came."

The car stopped, this being the end of the road in this direction, and they alighted, compelled to pick their way forward on foot for some distance. Leadley restrained Joan, and kept her at the rear of the party.

Deep in the heart of the jungle, and some three feet to the side of a pathway, lying half-hidden in the wet grass, was the body of Richard Sargent. It was plain, at the first glance, that he was dead. A little cordon of police was there, but following orders, everyone had stayed carefully back.

Sargent lay half on his side, his face only partly exposed. It was evident at a glance that he had been dead for many hours. There was no blood on him.

Joan Sargent saw, and gave a stifled cry. Leadley picked her up, unresisting, in his arms, carried her back to the car and drove back to the hotel.

Hearle studied the surroundings for a few moments, then moved forward. Again he noted details carefully, but waited until Dr. Strait, who had been summoned, presently arrived. A swift examination was enough for the coroner.

"He was hit across the back of the neck with some heavy weapon, like a blackjack," he explained. "Hit from behind, without warning. The skin is scarcely broken, and there is no blood. But his neck was broken, and he died instantly."

CHAPTER IX.

Further investigation disclosed that Richard Sargent had been robbed. And therein both Critton and the police agreed as to the whole story.

"It's plain enough," Critton declared. "He murdered Kasmin—the motive there was plain enough, and no one else could have done it. Then, when he found that we were on his trail, and that things were getting too hot for him, he decided to skip out last night, while he had a chance. So he got the idea of jumping a train to get out of the city, and came down here, where he could take either a G. N. or N. P. train the easiest.

"When he came down here, of course he was dressed like a gentleman. Anyone could tell at a glance that he was prosperous. And some tramps, being pretty tough eggs, bumped him off, robbed him, and, I suppose, have made their get-away by now. We're holding the man who reported finding him, but it's not likely that he had anything to do with it."

"You make out a very clear case," Hearle observed. "Nothing wrong with it, on the face of it. But if we accept it, what becomes of your having him pull out in that airplane last night, and fly to Canada?"

"It's quite evident that he didn't do that. Though that would have been the logical way for him to do it, if he really wanted to get away."

"So it would have," Hearle agreed.

"But he probably got in a panic, lost his head, and tried this way," Critton amplified.

Hearle shook his head.

"He was the sort who never gets in a panic, never loses his head, no matter what comes up," he said. "He may have done all this, as you say, but if so, he did it deliberately."

The body was removed then, under the directions of the coroner, and taken back to town. The others returned to their car.

"I suppose you will put out a general drag-net and round up all the transients?" Hearle inquired.

"It's already started, and we have notified neighboring cities," Critton nodded. "The trouble is, that we have so little evidence to go on, with any-one picked up somewhere else—and the chances are ten to one that whoever did it is a long way from Helena by now. Of course, some of Sargent's money or personal possessions might be found on some tramp. That's about our only hope."

During the next few hours, though on the surface he appeared to do very little, Eric Hearle was really very busy. Just before lunch time, Critton called him up to explain a development which left the prosecutor jubilant.

"I think that we're really beginning to get somewhere now," he declared. "Our round-up has been a pretty thorough one this morning, and it has brought in one character who ties up with this case, or I miss my guess. He gives his name as Bill Kurz, and claims to be from Nebraska, but Sheriff Oliver mighty soon got the goods on him. He's really Jake Napoli, one of Chicago's most notorious

gunmen, and a wire from the Chicago police tells
us that he was in one of the gangs most bitterly
opposed to Kasmin. Want to come and question
him?"

"I'll be right up," Hearle agreed. "Where is
he? At the county jail?"

"Yes. Shall I send a car, or will you take a
taxi?"

"Neither," decided Hearle. "I'll walk."

He proceeded to do so, enjoying the brisk blocks
up the hill. He found Critton awaiting him at the
court house, lounging on the steps, and together
they crossed over to the jail. Sheriff Oliver reported that, confronted with finger-prints, the
prisoner had confessed to being Jake Napoli of Chicago.

Napoli was a small man, dark, with gleaming
eyes under a huge shock of hair, a twisted nose
and vulpine mouth. In all, he had the look of a
rat, though now he appeared quite at ease—in fact,
he seemed to feel at home in his present surroundings.

"You guys ain't got nothin' on me," he assured
them pleasantly. "What if Chi does know who I
am? They got plenty more like me, right there
now, that they don't know what to do with. Fact
is, they're damn glad to have me outa there, and
they ain't goin' to have you send me back for no
homecomin' week. So you might just as well let
me go. I'm on a vacation, see, and I ain't pullin'
any work in this burg o' yours. Just let me go,
and I'll hit the cinders on out."

"We didn't nab you for Chicago, in the first
place," Critton told him. "We picked you up for

79

our own entertainment. When did you hit town?"

"Just last night, and even that was an accident. I was on a freight, and me private car got in late. Stopped a long time, and I was feeling tired of riding, so I thought I'd just look around a little."

"Ever hear of John Kasmin?"

"You don't mean Nick Kasmin, of Chi?"

"Maybe that's what he was called. A big shot there, I understand. He left the city a few months ago."

"Yeh, I've heard of him, all right. It got too hot for Nick, and so he got out while the gettin' was good."

"Then you hadn't heard that he was murdered here, the night before last?"

"Say, what you givin' me, anyway? Nick Kasmin bumped? Who'd do it?"

"That's what we're interested in finding out," Critton retorted grimly. "And we're likewise interested in the fact that you happen to be in town, right now. It seems rather odd that your private car should come here at such a time. I suppose you can furnish proof that you came in here last night, and not the night before?"

"Who? Me? Say, Mister, how in blazes would I furnish any proof, knockin' around this country the way I been doin'? But I didn't blow in to your burg till last night, and if I'd known you had a rap like this waitin' for me, I sure wouldn't have got off my parlor car none."

"Well, if you didn't kill Kasmin, did you kill anybody last night?"

Napoli turned around in amazement.

"Say, bo, what yuh givin' me? You talk like

bumpin' somebody every day was a regular thing with me. I may have bumped a guy or so in my day, back in Chi—maybe. But it ain't a habit with me, or nothin' like that."

"You didn't wrap a lead pipe around a gentleman's skull, down in the jungle, last night, then?"

"I didn't, no. But darn it, this ain't what I figured it was at all. Here I think you're just holdin' me as a suspicious character, gettin' ready to float me. But if you're tryin' to accuse me of murder, then I ain't talkin' none, see? I'm gettin' me a lawyer, instead."

"Get yourself a lawyer, if you like," Critton shrugged. "There's no murder charge against you—yet, but there may be. We're holding you here for investigation for a while." He turned to Hearle. "You can ask him anything you like."

"Thanks, but you seem to have covered the ground very well," Hearle returned.

Critton turned back to Napoli.

"If you know anything, you'd better tell it," he warned. "You'll get off easier that way."

"Me, I'm not talkin' only through my lawyer from now on," Napoli grunted.

"I'm pretty sure he had something to do with murdering Sargent last night," Critton worried. "He's just the sort who would be mixed up in that. And he had a big roll on him when he was arrested, which is mighty suspicious, considering that he was riding the rods—or claimed to be. The two don't go together very well. It looks to me as though he rode a freight train into town, like he says, then bumped Sargent off. He's just the kind who would do that. The only trouble is,

81

we have nothing to go by in identifying the money, unless we are lucky enough to find some of Sargent's finger-prints on the bills. Oliver is working on that now. Napoli didn't have anything else on him that he might have taken off Sargent, but then, he would be shrewd enough to throw other things away, of course."

"There may be some connection," Hearle agreed. "Anyway, it will do no harm to hold him for a few days. I want to question the tramp who discovered Sargent now."

Critton led the way to another cell. But it was obvious to Hearle from the first, that this man knew nothing more than he had told. He had been moving along the path, a bit bleary-eyed, as he confessed, from indulging in a dose of canned heat the night before, and had been startled nearly out of his wits by discovering the body lying there in the grass. He had stopped stock still in his tracks, sobered by the sight. Then, quelling his natural impulse to flee, he had done the proper thing and promptly reported his find.

"I think he's telling the truth," Critton agreed. "Though it will do no harm to hold him a little longer."

"He can doubtless stand a few free meals," Hearle nodded.

Returning to the hotel, Hearle was met in the lobby by the clerk, who drew him aside.

"In view of all the strange things that have been happening around here lately, I thought that you should know of this, Mr. Hearle," he explained. "There was something rather odd that happened last night, though so far as I can see, it could have no connection with other events. I'll let Mrs. Jones tell her own story, however. Will you kindly step back into the office for a moment?"

There Hearle found Mrs. Jones herself waiting—a rather plump, nervous, but motherly appearing old lady.

"I'll tell it to you just as it happened, Mr. Hearle," she agreed. "Last evening, I had been out to a restaurant for supper—I never can remember the names of these places—but anyway, it was good food. Afterwards I came back, and took the elevator up, and went down the hall to my room. When I went out for supper, I left it locked, like I always do. I had my key in my hand-bag, but when I tried to put it in the key-hole, it wouldn't go in. So I called a bell-boy, and he tried it. But he couldn't get it either, so he called the night-clerk, and he worked at it a while. We finally got the door open. The queer thing about it was, that there was another key on the inside, which kept my key from going in like it was supposed to."

"Was anything disturbed in your room?" Hearle demanded with a trace of excitement.

"I could tell that somebody had been in there, all right," Mrs. Jones nodded complacently. "They'd tried to leave everything as it had been, but you can't fool *me* that way. Everything seemed to be all right, though, and I haven't been able to find that anything was stolen. I was kind of nervous, but nothing bothered me during the night."

"I should like to have a look up there, if I may," Hearle decided.

"Certainly," agreed the clerk. "And there is

one other thing that happened last night—between nine and ten, I think it was, the lights on that side of the hotel went out for a few minutes. Several patrons complained, but by the time we could investigate, they went on again, and we decided there must have been a short-circuit somewhere. But I thought it best to tell you."

CHAPTER X.

Hearle stepped to the phone, called up the deputy prosecutor, and requested his presence at the hotel. A few minutes later, breathless, Critton hurried in.

"I had just sat down to lunch," he confessed, "but I left it without eating a mouthful. Have you found something new?"

"That remains to be seen," Hearle replied. "I'm sorry to have disturbed your lunch. I had forgotten all about it, myself."

Accompanied by the clerk and Mrs. Jones, they stepped into the elevator, and were let out, as Hearle noted, on the same floor as were the rooms that had been occupied by Richard Sargent. Down the hall, past these, the clerk led the way, to a room on the opposite side and at the end of the hall. This room, as Hearle noted, was one of the less desirable rooms of the hotel. There were several of these, as big and comfortable as any, but with windows fronting on a narrow alley, not over seven feet wide, a narrow canyon between two large buildings. Besides, at the far end, this alley ended against a third building, so that it was dark at the street level even at midday, and the only entrance was on a narrow side-street.

"At what hour did you return to your room last night, Mrs. Jones?" Hearle inquired.

"About a quarter to ten, I think it was."

"And how long was it before you were able to get into your room, after returning?"

85

"About fifteen minutes, I'd say."

"The lights were on in your room when you did enter it?"

"Oh, yes. They didn't give me any trouble."

"You had—er, rather a late supper?"

"Well, I did take in a movie afterward. 'Hearts Aflame,' I think it was."

"I see. By the way," turning to the clerk, "were all the lights on this side of the building out at the same time?"

"They appeared to be. At least, those on the four lower floors were. You see, sir, now that I come to think of it, the lighting arrangement on this side is a bit antiquated—older than that of the rest of the hotel. The lights on this side could be turned on or off by means of a switch."

"Without affecting the other lights?"

"Yes."

"Very interesting." And that building across the alley—what is it?"

"An old storehouse of some sort, I think. Furniture, perhaps—I scarcely know."

"Not used much then, at night?"

"Hardly at all, I believe."

"And no windows fronting on the alley. A very nice, quiet dark place indeed, between nine and ten o'clock last night—especially after some one had had the forethought to turn that switch on this side of the hotel for a little while."

Hearle glanced out of the window again. The fire escape, he saw, started at the far side of the building, and did not make a direct connection with this window at all. However, a drop of some eight feet would bring one down to it, and from there the distance to the ground was only some twenty feet.

"Let's go out and look around in the alley, Critton," Hearle suggested briskly. "Looks nice and muddy."

The alley was indeed muddy, a few little pools of water still standing in it. Thinking back, Hearle knew that it had stopped raining at around ten o'clock the night before—accordingly, just a few minutes after whoever had occupied the alley had left there, and probably somewhat to his chagrin.

Using a flash-light, Hearle studied the street at the entrance to the alley—narrow, unpaved, with an old ash can spilling out its contents through a crack in the side. A deserted, lonely place at night, though scarcely more than a stone's throw removed from the heart of the city.

Evidence of something having occurred here recently was plain to see in the mud, which was very deep and soft. A double pair of thin tracks, like those of buggy-wheels, ran down the alley, to pause almost directly below the fire escape. The tracks of a horse, and those of two or three men—all formless in the mud, but all, beyond a doubt, made just a little while before the rain had stopped the night before.

"What do you make of it?" Critton asked, doubtfully. "It looks like a horse and buggy had come in here, though why they should want to is beyond me. Besides that, how on earth could they turn around in here? Or did they back in here? It's a long way from the street."

"They backed the buggy in here, yes," Hearle

agreed. "They unhitched the horse—it must have been only a single-horse rig, you see, and an old one at that, judging by the wobbly tracks of the wheels—back at the street. Then the men—two of them, also, I think—pushed the buggy back in here by hand. After that, they hitched the horse up again and it drew the buggy out. You will notice that the tracks of the horse run quite evenly, in the middle of the wheel tracks, going out, also that the wheel tracks run straight. The wheel tracks are wobbly, coming in, when it was being pushed, and the horse was led more at the side."

"That's right," agreed Critton. "But what the devil is it all about, anyway? Why should they do all of that?"

"As to what it's all about, the buggy was used to carry off the dead body of Richard Sargent."

Critton fell back a step, staring in open-mouthed amazement. He leaned up against the far wall of the alley as if for support.

"Will you please say that again?"

"It's all quite clear enough," Hearle replied. "Let's get out of here, get our shoes cleaned up, and go inside again. Then I'll tell you about it. H'm. All they had to do was to drive for half a block, then they struck some paving, and of course all trace of the wheels was lost. Not that it matters."

He led the way back into the hotel and up to his own rooms. There he sank wearily into a chair.

"I asked the clerk to have some lunch sent up," he explained. "Ah, here it comes now. We may combine business with pleasure for a few minutes, at any rate."

Not until the waiter had spread their meal on a small table, and departed, did he explain.

"It was at once obvious to me, this morning, that Richard Sargent had not been murdered down in what you call the jungle. One glance satisfied me of that fact. In the first place, the path was muddy, from the rain of last night, and the heavy rain of the night before. The footprints of the tramp who discovered Sargent's body were very plain to see, thanks to your foresight in ordering that no one should approach the body until our arrival.

"The tramp had been walking along the path, and happened to glance to the side and discover the body in the tall grass. He stopped stock still, instantly, and remained frozen in his tracks for a space of seconds. It must have been quite a shock to him. None the less, he showed that he had a logical mind, in that crisis. He did not molest the body or do anything to spoil the evidence that might exist, or in any way implicate himself. He studied it out, standing all the time at least six feet away from the body, since it lay some three feet off the path, in the high grass. Then the tramp backed away and came and told what he knew. You may as well release him. He rendered a very real service, and deserves a reward rather than jail.

"No one else, as I could see, had been anywhere near there since it stopped raining. Someone—probably two men—had been down that path some few minutes before the rain stopped last night, for their tracks were only partly washed out. They came down the path, bearing a heavy burden in their arms, as the deeper tracks denote. The prints made by their shoes were filled with water this morning. It doesn't take much rain, you know, when the ground is thoroughly soaked, to seep into such depressions.

"Their burden, plainly, was the body of Sargent. Without stopping or making any extra tracks, they threw him from them, so that his body fell in the grass beside the pathway, precisely as we saw it this morning. Then they went on again, the rain washing away all evidence, yet their tracks from there on were not nearly so deep in the mud.

"Their intention, I judge, was to make it appear that he had been doing what you assumed—walking there, seeking perhaps to board a train, and that he had been murdered and robbed by some tramp. Though there again they overlooked two important points.

"If a tramp had slugged him, he might, of course, have hit him from behind, but the chances are ten to one that he would have hit him over the head, and so hard as to break the skin, and crush the skull—in which case, there would have been a lot of blood. But there was no blood. He was hit on the back of the neck, a carefully calculated, murderous blow, which broke the neck and killed instantly without causing blood. Only an expert could have achieved such a result.

"And then, having thrown his body down by the pathway, in their very natural nervousness, they forgot to trample up things, to make it look as though there had been a hold-up, murder, or robbery, there. Or very likely they counted on the rain keeping on and washing away all evidence of any sort. In that, they were fooled."

90

Critton looked foolish.

"That's all true, now that you point it out to me," he admitted. "You must think I'm awfully dumb."

"Not dumb. You merely lack training along those lines," Hearle commented. "And, as I have suggested before, you jump at conclusions too quickly."

"All that being so," Critton admitted humbly, "I still don't get it, or understand why they would take his body down there. Where was he killed, and how?"

"He was killed in his own rooms, as he entered them last night, after coming back from the Dearborn with Mr. Leadley. He went up to his rooms to clean and dress for dinner, as he told Mr. Leadley. Unfortunately for him, his daughter was nowhere around at the time, and whoever killed him was fully aware of the fact, knew that the coast was clear. The murderer had let himself into Mr. Sargent's rooms, probably after overhearing him tell Mr. Leadley that he was going up to them. As soon as Sargent entered, and before he could turn the lights on, he was struck that one fatal blow from behind, with some heavy object. Who did it, or why, we do not know. But whoever killed Mr. Kasmin also killed Mr. Sargent. Both were cases of carefully planned murder.

"Mr. Sargent was dead before he even suspected that he was being attacked. But the murderer had no desire to leave him there, in his own room. He preferred to make the whole thing more intricate, to confuse us in every way possible. It reminds me in that part, of the case to which I referred the other

91

night, of the Van Horn sister and her husband being killed, and its being made to look like the work of Chinese thugs—oh, pardon me, you were not present when I told of that, were you? However, no matter. The murderer failed to befuddle us very well merely because it happened to stop raining."

"But how did he do it—get the body out and all?"

"There were, as we have discovered, two of them. They had taken pains to familiarize themselves very thoroughly with the hotel and its surroundings. The crime, of course, was planned in advance. It must have taken place at around eight-thirty. They then proceeded to get the horse and buggy ready in the alley below—in fact, it would look as though there were more than two, to do all of this—then they turned out the lights on that side of the hotel, went through Mrs. Jones' room, lowered the body through the window to the fire escape and so into the buggy. Driving down to the jungle, they carried the body off on that path and dropped it. All this took time, of course. And every time element fits very nicely together."

CHAPTER XI.

The house of High Sing crouches back against a pock-marked hill of Last Chance Gulch itself; pock-marked by the efforts of men mad with the lust for gold, who had burrowed like puny gophers into the sides of the mountains, seeking to wrest yellow treasure from them. These old prospect holes, diggings, are everywhere along the gulch, but nowhere more numerous than near to and behind the house of High Sing. The city of Helena had its beginnings here. But the modern city spreads down the gulch to the northward, and overflows on to the hills and plains.

This house of High Sing, Hearle noted, was an ancient frame dwelling, long and rather dark, decrepit with age. In its recesses, however, High Sing and his family lived; moreover, they conducted a more or less prosperous laundry business. High Sing had reported to the police that his laundry wagon was missing; had been stolen the previous evening.

Critton, who had already set an inquiry afoot, and to whom the news of this theft was immediately reported, had turned to Hearle in excitement.

"That's the buggy we're looking for," he declared. "I've seen it occasionally. It must be almost as old as I am, maybe more. It is an old buggy High Sing got hold of for his laundry business. He built some sort of a long, low body on it,

93

and has his grandson drive it now for delivering laundry, with an old brown, moth-eaten horse that must have come out of the ark. It answers the description in every way."

While Critton busied himself with trying to find the old buggy itself, Hearle picked his way up into Chinatown and knocked on High Sing's door. The old man was wizened and yellow as parchment, shrunken more into the semblance of a mummy than that of a man. He was still active, however, ceremoniously polite, and he talked fairly good English.

"I came to ask you about your missing laundry wagon," Hearle explained. "And to tell you that the police are making every effort to find it."

High Sing shot him a sharp glance from under rather scanty brows, and rubbed his leathery hands together.

"You be detective, work on this murder case," he declared. "You think also that my wagon caught up in it, some way. The police not be so much interested in find wagon for High Sing, by itself."

"You're quite right," Hearle admitted. "We think there may be some connection."

High Sing moved to a door, spoke rapidly in a harsh guttural for a few moments, returned, and sank into a chair.

"I call my grandson, Charley. He driving wagon last night. He tell you about it. Charley," he added, "he velly much American boy."

A moment later Charley High entered the room. He was a lad of about twelve, and save for his Oriental features, he might easily have been mistaken for any American boy about the city, both in speech

94

and manner, as well as dress. Just now, however,
he appeared rather pale.

"You tell him what you know about wagon,
Charley," High Sing admonished.

"Well, it was this way, sir. I have been driving
that old buggy for a couple of years now, after
school hours and so on, to do the delivering. Last
night, after school, I started out as usual, and I
had to go around quite a bit——out near the capital,
down into the N. P. section, and so on. It took
me quite a while to get around, for that old crowbait that granddad calls a horse ain't what you'd
call speedy. So it was dark and raining before
I got ready to go home.

"I was pretty anxious to get back, for I was
wet and hungry, so I came straight up Main Street.
It's the shortest way back, and of course, being
paved, it wasn't muddy. Usually I stay off it
with that rig, on account of traffic, but last night
there wasn't much going on, so I followed it.

"I was just a little ways past the Last Chance
Hotel when a man called to me from the sidewalk,
and wanted to rent the horse and buggy——"

"Just a moment," interposed Hearle. "What
did this man look like?"

"Let's see. Well, he was rather tall, pretty well
tanned, with sort of a cold face. He was wearing
a cap too, and I think his hair was brown. He had
a crisp, short way of speaking, like he was used to
giving orders. And he had on high leather boots.
too, like swells wear, and sort of hiking clothes,
though they weren't just the common sort."

Hearle nodded. Charley High had drawn a remarkably accurate picture of Pinard, he reflected.

"Go on," he said.

"Well, he seemed to like the looks of the old wreck I was driving, for some reason or other. Muttered to himself once or twice that it was just the thing. Then he asked me if I would rent it or sell it to him. I asked him what he wanted it for, and he said he thought he could use it. I got to thinking afterward maybe he did have something in mind, especially after what happened later. But right then I was cold and hungry, and I couldn't see what anybody would want of such an old wreck, 'specially at bed time. I thought he was kidding me, and I guess I wasn't very polite. I told him to go jump in the lake, and drove on."

"Ah. And what did he do?"

"I don't know. I didn't look back to see. But when I got up in this part of town I turned off to go through an alley, that I always follow to the barn, and a couple of men with masks on jumped out from the dark side of the alley fence. One of them grabbed the horse by the bit, the other jumped up on the buggy wheel, grabbed me, and hit me over the head with a club or something, before I knew what was going on. When I woke up, a couple of hours later I guess it was, I was lying there, kind of in the shelter of an old shed, and my head ached awfully. You can see the bump on it yet."

He parted his hair, disclosing a bump. Hearle nodded sympathetically. It was evident that whoever had struck the blow had not hit gently.

"Can you describe either of the men who ambushed you? Was either of them the man who had accosted you on the street before, do you think?"

"Looked to me like one of them might have been the same guy," Charley admitted. "But it was pretty dark there, and I didn't have a chance for much of a look. Besides, as I say, they was both wearin' masks then."

"Would it have been possible for the man who stopped you first, to be one of them, do you think?"

"Oh, sure. All he'd have had to do would be to jump in a car, follow me up a little, see where I was going, take another street and get ahead, and I'd never have known it. Plenty of time and chance. At the rate that old crowbait moves, he could have done it on foot if he'd cared to move along a little."

"You didn't notice anything else that might be suspicious, at any time last evening?"   ?

"Well, now I come to think of it, I did. When that first fellow stopped me to ask about rentin' the buggy—"

"Just a moment," interrupted Hearle. "You say that was just a little way above the Last Chance Hotel?"

"Yes. He was standin' on the street, right about at Main and Edwards, I remember. And what I started to say was, he seemed to have a partner with him, waitin' there on the street corner. I didn't pay much attention to him then, or think much about it till just now. But I guess he did have a partner, all right."

"And was he another big man?"

"He might have been. I can't be sure."

"Well, I'm much obliged for the information," Hearle declared, "and we'll try and get your laundry wagon back." He paused for a few moments to look over the laundry, to ask a few questions, mostly for the sake of politeness. High Sing declared that he was an old man—just how old, he didn't know. He had been born in an alley in Canton; at the age of ten he had managed to stow away on a ship bound for San Francisco, the land of gold. Discovered on the second day out, he had been soundly whipped and put to work.

Arriving many weeks later, he had found the new land to be singularly lacking in gold, and had finally drifted to Helena. There, as he explained, he had likewise failed to find gold, but he had been there for well over half a century.

"You come see me again," he invited. " I make you dish noodles like they make in China." Seeing Hearle's look of doubt, he smiled, rubbed his hands together, and added:

"They not like the noodles, chop suey, you buy Chinese restaurant in this country. No, no. Noodles in China different—better. And chop suey—that American dish, not Chinese. Made here for Americans, not made in China. No. You come some time, I send Charley."

So Hearle agreed. Back at his hotel, he found Critton, but, remembering his fondness for jumping to conclusions and arresting someone on the slightest provocation, he did not tell him all that he had learned. Time enough for that if the further evidence pointed in the same way.

Critton, however, reported that the police had succeeded in finding High Sing's laundry wagon, about a mile below the jungle, down in the diggings. The horse was still attached to it when found, peacefully grazing on such vegetation as it could find. The wagon appeared to have suffered no damage.

Together they looked it over carefully. There was every indication that it had been used to carry the body of Richard Sargent from the alley to the jungles, but of more direct evidence as to who had done it, there was nothing at all.

Back in his own rooms again, Hearle surveyed his shoes rather dubiously. He enjoyed walking, preferred it to riding when posible, but there had been a lot of mud up in Chinatown, and the shoes showed it. He rang for the porter.

That gentleman presently appeared, of ebony hue and with a wide grin as he surveyed the shoes.

"Yas sah, boss, I shuah fixes them up bright's a new dollah fo yo," he declared. "This makes the second paiah of right muddy shoes I has to clean to-day. Another gemman calls me in this mo'nin and asks me can I clean up his, or had he bettah throw them in the gahbage can. They was sho pow'ful muddy, too. Sticky mud, clean ovah the tops. Gemman said he'd been out walkin' last night, climbed Mount Helena, he said, so as to get the view good of the city at night. Made me wondah, did he look at it through a bottle, maybe, widout doin' no climbin'. But I shuah fixed his boots up nice, and he give me a dollah."

"Here's a dollar in advance," Hearle smiled. "You say he was another gentleman from this hotel?"

"Yes sah, boss, thank you sah, he was. Tall

99

gentleman, name of Mr. Pinney, I think it was.
One o' these heah movie men."

"Oh, Mr. Pinard, eh?   And his boots were all
muddy?"

"Muddy's all get out, sah.   Mighty fine boots,
and high ones, too, but he must have been just
wallowin' in mud.   Said he slipped once, comin'
down 'at mountain, and slid a ways.   Man, it sho
did look it. But ah'll fix these shoes o' yo's up
so's yo'll nevah know they knew what mud is, yas
sah, boss."

CHAPTER XII

"I hate to trouble you now, Miss Sargent," Hearle told Joan, genuine sympathy vibrating in his voice. "But it seems to me that there is a missing link somewhere, in the relations between your father and Mr. Kasmin. I want to find out who murdered your father. And since they were both, apparently, struck down by the same hand, it seems to me that anything which they may have had in common—have even discussed together, you understand—might tend to throw light on it all."

Joan, very pale but composed now, with Elinor Ferguson hovering nearby, watching her as though she had been a sister, nodded thoughtfully.

"I'll tell you all I know," she agreed. "Though I can't think that any of it is important. Father, as I think you know, was a widely traveled man. He had spent a great many years, off and on, in China. He—"

"A moment, please, Miss Sargent. You were with him on some of those trips to China, I imagine?"

"Yes, I have been there three or four times. I was born in China, in fact."

"That is interesting. And your mother, if I may inquire—?"

"She died when I was a small child. We were in the Philippines at the time, and she contracted a fever."

"Did your father ever seem to have any special reason for being in China—any mission, business, or anything like that?"

"I think he did, yes. He had a hobby, you see—

101

two hobbies, in fact. The chief one was the collection of rare Chinese daggers."

"I suppose you were interested in his hobby
as well?"

Joan shrugged slightly.

"Not in that one. I hated the things. They
always seemed so suggestive of nameless evil to me."

"Then you knew very little about his collection?"

"Yes. I scarcely ever looked at them."

"I understand. And his other hobby—his mission?"

"I wouldn't call it a mission, exactly. He
seemed to be very much interested in people, always.
The odder they were, the more difficult to understand, the better it pleased him."

"Then you would say that he seemed to have
no special reason for going—anywhere?"

"None, except his liking for travel. You see,
the shock of my mother's death was a great one
to him, and he tried to forget, through travel.
Although, of course, business occasionally called
him back to this country. He had investments on
the Pacific coast, which was the reason for our
present trip to this country. We had spent last
winter in Egypt, you see. And on this trip we
again met Mr. Leadley, and were invited to join
this party and visit a real dude ranch." She smiled
faintly.

"Pray go on. I have hindered you in answering
my original question."

"Well, we had a few days to knock around in
California, before coming up here, and it wasn't
long before father headed for San Francisco. I
knew that he would, and just where he would go

when he got there—to Chinatown. He had done so every time we visited the coast. He has many friends in Chinatown, of course."

"And he was looking for anything new in the way of his collection, doubtless?"

Joan sighed, roused from a momentary fit of abstraction.

"I suppose so. Anyway, we went to a little restaurant at midday, called the Roses of Fragrant Gardens, and while we were there, who should come in but Mr. Kasmin and Miss Dixon. That was the first time that we had ever seen Mr. Kasmin, but we had known Miss Dixon before, and seeing us, she came up, introduced Mr. Kasmin, and they joined us at our table.

"I'm going to tell you just what happened there, though I can't think that there was anything important to it. We dawdled through the meal so that it was a rather long one. Toward the close of it, a little door opened and a big Chinaman came in. Most of the Chinese down there, you know, are not very big—they are the typical Chinese that we see over in this country, I might say. But this fellow, who was about forty-five, was a splendid physical specimen. He must have been from somewhere in the northern interior of China, where they have big men as a rule—stalwart giants, well over six feet. They can take a pack of three hundred and fifty pounds on their backs and walk off with it, and go at a steady stride nearly all day long. This man was like them.

"He had not been in this country very long, I judged, for he could scarcely speak English at all. I'm not sure, but I thought that my father must know this man. He gave him a quick, odd look, although he didn't say anything, either then or later, and after it was over, I forgot to ask him. But that was the impression that I gathered, though I may be wrong.

"Anyway, this big giant came up to the table where we were seated, and my father evidently expected him to speak to him. But instead of that, the Chinaman made us understand that he wanted to speak to Mr. Kasmin, in private. He had a hard time making us understand even that much, for he spoke very poor English. Once he turned, rather helplessly, to the proprietor, a very old and wrinkled Cantonese, and fired several words at him in Chinese—an appeal for help, I think. But the proprietor shook his head. He couldn't understand.

"But father did. He is very well educated in the principal Chinese dialects, and he said that the man spoke Mandarin, the more cultured tongue of North China. It is more soft and fluid than the tongue of South China. Though they both read and write the same language, one from the North cannot understand one from the South. Father understood both the main dialects very well, however, and spoke them passably well.

"So he explained to Mr. Kasmin that this man, Mr. Pin H'sueh, wished to see Mr. Kasmin on a matter of business in private for a moment. Mr. Kasmin evidently knew the fellow, and he didn't seem very well pleased to see him, but after a moment he got up and went into a little side room with him.

"They tried to talk for a minute or so, I guess, but couldn't make a go of it, for pretty soon they both came back and asked father to act as interpreter for them. So he did. They all three went back in that little room and stayed for perhaps ten minutes. Then they came out again, and Mr. Pin went off. Father looked rather grave, and Mr. Kasmin mopped his face with a handkerchief, as though he had come through a hard ordeal."

"You have no idea as to what they were talking about, Miss Sargent?"

"None. Father never mentioned the affair at all. The next day, however, as our whole party was getting on the train to come to Montana, Mr. Kasmin happened to be standing near us, and he looked off in the direction of Chinatown and said that he was damned glad to be getting out of this Chinese nest, and would be thankful to get a long way from it.

"Father looked at him, and shrugged a little, with contempt, I think."

"'There may be safer places, Kasmin,' he replied. 'Though the yellow tongs have a long arm.'"

"I have wondered," Joan added, "if that reference to the yellow tongs could have anything to do with their deaths here. For there is a Chinatown here, too, and father has referred to safety. First, Mr. Kasmin was killed, then father—and they had both discussed the same thing in that room with Mr. Pin H'sueh."

"It's certainly worth looking into," Hearle agreed. "And we will do so."

In this belief, Critton heartily concurred, once the gist of the conversation was repeated to him.

"It gives us an entirely new angle to work from," he said thoughtfully. But this affair has already been connected up with Chinatown last

105

night, and this seems to mix it up more than ever.
We'll put a dragnet up in Chinatown next, and see
what we can bring in."

Meanwhile, as a little of the afternoon yet remained Hearle determined to spend it in pursuing the
same clue a little further. With this thought in mind,
he sought out Mrs. Reid.

"History," Hearle smiled, "is said to repeat itself, and scholars assure us that we may judge the
future by the past. At any rate, in an investigation such as this, I have found it valuable to know
something of the past of those involved. You,
as I understand it, Mrs. Reid, have been acquainted
with several members of this party, more or less,
for a number of years. So naturally I come to you."

"You consider me a gossip who loves to wag
her tongue," Mrs. Reid replied. "Well, perhaps
you are close to the truth. Anyway, I'll be glad to
help you if I can. Whose shady past is to be
turned up to the light of day?"

"I was thinking principally, at the moment, of
our two victims."

"Poor men." Mrs. Reid shuddered. "I always
feel so—so horribly guilty, when I think of them,
after speaking to you as I did the other night, and
hoping for a murder. Everything seems to have
started to happen right after that. As to Mr.
Kasmin, I've already told you all I know. With
Mr. Sargent I might be able to go back a few years.
Yes, I can go back five or six, in his relations with
Mr. Pinard, if you are interested. Since Mr. Pinard
is above suspicion, I see no harm in letting my
tongue wag if it will entertain you."

"Please do, Mrs. Reid. Five or six years, eh?"

"About that. I knew them both then, more or less. Less, I suppose I may as well confess. So most of what I have to tell you is largely hearsay, but reasonably accurate, I think. That was before Mr. Pinard was married, but not many months. They had business relations together then, I think— Mr. Pinard and Mr. Sargent. Anyway, as I heard it, they had bought up an old, abandoned gold mine, somewhere out there in California—I never was any good at remembering names of places— believing that, by the use of modern machinery, the mine could be worked some more and made to pay well. As I understood it, they each put a hundred thousand dollars into the proposition. That wasn't a great sum for Mr. Sargent, but I guess it was a lot for Mr. Pinard in those days. He wasn't very rich then, as he is now.

"And for the first few months, things didn't go at all well with their investment. They had sunk their whole two hundred thousand, and hadn't found anything but dirt. Every indication was, that they could keep right on sinking money, but wouldn't be apt to get any out again.

"It was about then that their relations became rather strained, I think, over Dolores Dixon. She was a beauty, even then, and though she wasn't much older than Mr. Sargent's own daughter, Joan, of course that wouldn't necessarily make much difference, with a man like him, not old at all, really, and who had been a widower for many years."

"You mean that he wanted to marry Miss Dixon?" Hearle interjected.

"Well, that was what everybody thought, including Mr. Pinard. At any rate, Mr. Sargent seemed to take a great deal of interest in Miss Dixon, whom Mr. Pinard regarded as his own find, and I guess, as his own personal property. Anyway, he resented Mr. Sargent's interest in her, bitterly, and that led, I am convinced, to their break in other ways.

"Of course, Mr. Pinard had no more money to invest in their mine. So, as I heard it, Mr. Sargent bought Mr. Pinard out, giving him back just what he had put into it—a hundred thousand dollars. I suppose that Mr. Pinard thought he was lucky to get out of it without a loss, at the time.

"But it wasn't a week, after Mr. Pinard had sold out, before a new rich vein of gold was struck in the mine. I suppose that added to Mr. Pinard's bitterness, and some say that Mr. Sargent had known of the gold all the time, and kept it covered up until Mr. Pinard was out of the mine. The discovery of it so very soon after Mr. Pinard had sold out, without spending any more money for development, would make it look suspicious. Though I don't believe that, for Mr. Sargent wasn't that sort. Besides, by that time, Mr. Pinard had married Miss Dixon, and Mr. Sargent and his daughter had already sailed off for Japan or somewhere. The mine, they say, has paid Mr. Sargent two or three million dollars since then."

"A fortunate investment for him, certainly."

"It surely was. Though I imagine that Mr. Pinard, while he may have felt bitter, was better pleased to have Miss Dixon than the mine. And speaking in terms of wealth, her salary has paid them an amount at least equal to the mine, since then."

THE GOLDEN BOWL

Once started, Mrs. Reid chattered steadily on. But, though listening abstractedly for any further chance nugget of information, Hearle scarcely heard her. She told this, as she said, because there was nothing against Mr. Pinard. Nothing! All that had been lacking was the motive, and she had supplied that. What a motive! Jealousy, a bitterness of long years standing, a sense of wrong that would grow more bitter as he saw great wealth flowing into another man's pockets—wealth which he no doubt believed himself to have been cheated out of. Hearle shook his head, and, presently, strolled out into the street, feeling the need of fresh air to cope with this situation.

A horn squawked, rousing him from his abstraction. Hearle leaped nimbly as the car stopped with a squealing of brakes, then Dr. Strait stuck his head out and grinned.

"I almost added another patient to my string, then," he reproved. "But I suppose your head is full of the case, Mr. Hearle. However, don't get absent-minded in the middle of the street. Get in and go along with me a few minutes. I'm heading down to the N.P. section now."

"The N.P. eh?" Hearle glanced at his watch, and accepted. "I should like to meet the train from the east, now that I come to think of it. Senator Ferguson is expected in on it tonight."

"Senator Ferguson, eh? Mr. Leadley certainly had a distinguished company gathered together here, didn't he? Though they act very much like ordinary folks, in most ways—yourself, for instance, doing something so prosaic as almost to get run over. Which would have hurt both of us, for a

109

doctor isn't supposed to go out and make his own patients.

"And only the other day—Tuesday, I believe it was— the noon of the day that Kasmin was killed, anyway—I was passing by a noodle parlor up in Chinatown, and though I didn't recognize them at the time, I saw Mr. Sargent and the actress, Miss Dixon, in there, eating noodles together. Very much like ordinary folks under the skin, with the same likes and dislikes, the same primitive emotions, the same loves and hates. Mrs. O'Grady and the Colonel's lady. True, isn't it?"

"Pathetically so, sometimes," Hearle agreed.

CHAPTER XIII

The *Alaskan* ground to a stop, and passengers commenced to file down the steps along its length. Hearle, leisurely working his way along the station platform, discovered Leadley and the Ferguson girls, and made his way to them. A moment later he was being introduced to Senator Ferguson himself, was aware that he was undergoing the scrutiny of a pair of exceedingly sharp though friendly eyes.

Ferguson was a gray-haired man, a trifle above the medium in height, with a carefully trimmed beard somewhat after the fashion set by the King of England. Always quiet, self-possessed, he was acknowledged over the country to be one of the outstanding men in the United States Senate. Widely traveled, well informed, he was a man to reckon with on the floor; a man, Hearle decided, who would be a wonderful friend, and who could be, if necessary, a most unpleasant enemy.

It was not until they had arrived at the hotel that the Senator was given a brief resume of the tragic events of the past couple of days. The knowledge appeared to affect him profoundly. He questioned sharply, but made no comments at first.

"And Sargent's body?" he asked finally. "Where is it? I have heard of him many times in the course of the years; have possessed a curiosity to meet him. His death is a great shock to me, but I should like, at least, to look upon his face, if I may."

111

THE GOLDEN BOWL

"He is at a local funeral parlor," Leadley explained. "It has been decided that he shall rest in a local cemetery. Mr. Kasmin's body was sent back east today."

Hearle offered to guide the Senator, who promptly accepted the offer, and insisted that he wished to go at once, even before cleaning up and refreshing himself. In the lobby of the hotel, they encountered Louis Jouralmon and Mr. Critton. Hearle introduced them, and explained their present purpose.

"I'll join you, if I won't be intruding," Critton offered, and Jouralmon, deep in conversation with him before, also decided to go along.

The ride was a brief and silent one. At their destination, Ferguson stared down in silence for several moments at the impassive, handsome face of Richard Sargent, and shook his head.

"The Golden Bowl," he sighed. "Mr. Leadley had written me that he would be a member of this party, and I had heard of him many times in past years. I had heard also," he added, turning to the others directly, "that he had penetrated to a little known section of Mongolia, in the Amnyi Machen range—back among the Mountains of Mystery. Being somewhat of a student of that country myself, I had looked forward keenly to talking with him concerning that spot to which he penetrated. But I am, it seems, too late. The Golden Bowl is broken. And the gates of death never swing outward."

Again he turned, to stare down at Sargent's face, sighed as he turned away.

"May he rest in peace. But may his slayer be

112

imperfect in death, and so, as the Chinese say, never ascend the dragon throne. You have not arrested the guilty man?"

Hearle shrugged his shoulders.

"We've yet to find him," he confessed. "We have plenty of clues, but they point in too many directions. And so far we have no proof."

"I think that I may safely say, however, that we will have the guilty man arrested within twenty-four hours," Critton interjected. "I am looking forward to important developments yet this evening."

Senator Ferguson raised his eyebrows slightly, but made no comment. At the hotel again, Critton hurried to the phone, turned triumphantly back to Hearle.

"The police have found one strange Chinaman, who hasn't any good reason for being here, apparently. I knew they would. And the whole thing is bound to be solved up in Chinatown. Want to go with me to see him?"

"Of course," agreed Hearle.

As they went, Critton turned to Hearle with a slightly puzzled look on his face.

"Just what did the Senator mean about that Golden Bowl, and its being broken? Does he know something about this case?"

"He was referring, if I'm not mistaken, to the last chapter in the book of Ecclesiastes," Hearle explained.

"I'm afraid that leaves me still in the dark," Critton confessed. "I don't read the Bible a great deal."

"The Golden Bowl is merely a symbolical way

113

of speaking of death," Hearle added. "The Chinese speak of it as a black camel kneeling at your gate, and so on."

Hearle's interest in the Chinese, which had been very desultory, quickened at the sight of the new prisoner, who was being held for examination on some technical charge. He was a big man, with powerful shoulders, arms and hands, about forty-five, Hearle would have judged, utterly unlike most of his countrymen whom he had seen about the streets. Moreover, he had given his name as Pin H'sueh, of San Francisco.

He spoke English so poorly that it was almost impossible to understand him, and another Chinese called in as interpreter, explained that the newcomer must speak a Northern dialect, as he could not understand it at all. Here was something really tangible, Hearle felt. This was, unquestionably, the same man who had desired to see Kasmin in the Roses of Fragrant Gardens, in San Francisco's Chinatown—the man whom Kasmin had been afraid of, and concerning whom Sargent had remarked cryptically concerning the long arm of the tongs!

Mr. Pin, it developed, wrote Chinese fluently, and as the interpreter did likewise, here at last was a common meeting ground. Pin H'sueh protested that he was but in Helena to pay a visit to his esteemed cousin, Hung Lee. He had done nothing which merited investigation by the police.

"Ask him if his cousin, Hung Lee, speaks the same dialect that he does, and if he also speaks English," suggested Critton. "If so, we will have a direct interpreter."

But the interpreter paused; pulled thought-fully at his chin.

"Hung Lee," he repeated aloud. "I know a Lee Hung here, but I know of no Hung Lee, and I thought that I knew everyone of my own race in Helena."

He turned, scribbled a conglomeration of cryptic signs with astonishing swiftness and deftness on the pad, watched with beady eyes while Mr. Pin in turn did likewise, and repeated it. The others watched these meaningless symbols in tense silence. Finally the interpreter paused, spoke.

"We need other tablets," he said. "Come and help me get them, please."

Puzzled, they followed him out of the room. There he turned and spoke swiftly.

"He is shrewd as the very devil, this Pin H'sueh, and hard to trick," he declared. "Also, I think that he understands English, which is my reason for asking you to come out here. I asked him where Hung Lee lived, and he proceeded to explain that he was perhaps called Lee Hung in our dialect, and then explained where Lee Hung lived. He must have understood what you said to me. He added that he talked to Lee Hung through the writing, as we are doing. I think that he saw that he had come close to being trapped, and caught himself."

Critton nodded.

"I suspected he was up to something," he asserted.

"I know he is," the interpreter nodded. "For Lee Hung is a Cantonese man, as I am. I have talked with him many, many times. And he has told me that, because of a great flood, all of his people in China were swept away when he was a boy. He alone was left, without, so far as he could learn, a relative on earth."

Critton stepped to the phone.

"We will ask Lee Hung to come up and explain this to us," he said. "Sheriff Oliver will be glad to relay the request for us."

A few minutes later, having been found at his place of business, Lee Hung joined them. He was an aged, wrinkled little man, with a toothless grin. He listened serenely to the questions propounded, smiled and nodded.

"All that I told you was true, my good friend," he agreed. "True, so far as I knew. But mortal knowledge is limited. And Mr. Pin H'sueh has presented to me proofs that he is my blood cousin, but one time removed. A sister of my grandmother married an officer, who was attached to the staff of the Manchu governor of Canton. When in the course of political favors, which run like the waters of muddy streams, the governor returned north, so did his officer and his wife go with him. The record had been lost by my own people, but it was preserved in the north. Pin H'sueh had it all, and knowing that I was here somewhere, he carefully traced me when the opportunity was given, came to visit me, as a kinsman should."

"And when did he arrive?" Critton grunted.

Lee Hung pondered a moment.

"This is Thursday. He came on Tuesday morning, from the land of the setting sun."

"He speaks the Mandarin language, doesn't he?" Hearle asked quietly.

"Yes," agreed Lee Hung. "His father and his father's father were high officials under the Manchus. Of course they spoke the language of the court."

"Do you understand any of it?"

Lee Hung smiled and shook his head.

"I am an old man, and uneducated. I know only the dialect of Canton. But my cousin is an educated man, a fit and worthy son of officers of the Emperors of China."

"You are fully satisfied then, that he is your cousin?"

"I am satisfied."

"How long is he staying on this visit to you, Lee Hung?"

"He declared upon arrival that he could stay for one week in this city."

Hearle smiled.

"I suppose that, being of the rank he is, he feels the indignity of such an arrest and questioning as this, rather keenly, doesn't he?"

Lee Hung bowed.

"It is to be expected."

"Well," and Hearle leaned forward. "If you will give us your pledge that your cousin will not attempt to leave Helena until we give him permission to depart, and will be on hand to answer questions when we may desire to ask them, he can go free now. I will wish to question him to-morrow."

"My cousin will be most happy to do whatever you may desire," Lee Hung assured them.

Critton reluctantly gave the order for Pin

H'sueh's release. After they had gone he turned to Hearle.

"It looks foolish to me, to let them loose now," he declared. "I'm convinced that this Pin knows something about the case. He isn't up here just for a visit to a cousin he had never seen before."

"It's pronounced more like Bean, in the Chinese," Hearle replied pleasantly. "As to that, I quite agree with you, and I'm quite convinced that he knows more than he is telling. But I don't want him to get the idea that we really think he is of much importance. And I have no doubt that he will be safely on hand when we want him."

CHAPTER XIV

Pin H'sueh, comfortably lodged at the home of his cousin, Lee Hung, was smiling and affable on that sunny Friday morning, despite the earliness of the hour—for Hearle was early abroad, accompanied by Critton. Lee Hung, having welcomed the callers, proceeded to get paper and pencils, whereby to act as interpreter.

Hearle explained bluntly that he knew of that meeting betwen Pin H'sueh, Kasmin and Sargent, in the Roses of Fragrant Gardens, in San Francisco, and would Pin H'sueh be so obliging as to tell what really occurred in that inner room?

Pin H'sueh was happy, indeed, to be able to oblige. He had come that day, he explained, as the emissary of many leading citizens of Chinatown in San Francisco, to argue graciously with Mr. Kasmin and, if necessary, to give him a warning. Clear proof had been afforded himself and his honorable associates at their meeting, held the evening before, concerning the activities of Mr. Kasmin in their midst. Proof enough to satisfy anyone. Had Mr. Kasmin been a son of the Celestial Land, Pin H'sueh went on to explain, his actions would have been dealt with according to the ancient and honorable laws.

But being a white man, and this the country of the white man, they had chosen to act discreetly. In plain blunt words, Mr. Kasmin was a purveyor of the lotus flower—the sweet, fragrant, evil heart of the poppy, which gives dreams to its adherents of paradise, while plunging them down into the very gates of hell itself. In short, Kasmin was one of the higher-ups in a gigantic, nation-wide dope smuggling ring, which some of the leading Chinese, not themselves addicted to opium and hating it passionately, had been fighting for many, many years, in an endeavor to save their weaker-willed brothers.

This dope ring had its tentacles in the heart of China itself, and in many other countries. Pin H'sueh had fought it in China. A few short years before, he had come to America to continue the battle, equipped with special knowledge. And since Kasmin, having long been engaged in dope running as one part of his many activities, had been forced to take a vacation from Chicago, he had continued to work along that one line—as a higher-up—in San Francisco. But they had finally got the proof on him.

They did not choose, in the white man's land, to deal with him as he deserved, according to their own customs. But neither did they wish to turn him over to the white men to deal with according to their own laws. Pin H'sueh sighed. They had tried that method before, and the results had been regrettable. Equipped with highly paid lawyers who could twist black so that it looked like the shining colors of the rainbow, who could make an evil-smelling stench assume the pleasant frangrance of the costliest perfumes, those who had been indubitably guilty had gone free, but, warned, had placed themselves more or less surely beyond the reach of vengeance. So they could not allow Kasmin to be dealt with in this way.

Instead, they had chosen, through their most unworthy representative, Pin H'sueh himself, as a man with wide experience and with a bitter hatred of the poppy, to warn Kasmin to desist from his most regrettable practices. Mr. Sargent had proved to be of great value to Pin H'sueh, by acting as interpreter in the moment of need. Pin H'sueh had bungled that important matter, in making no adequate preparations in advance.

Yes, it was in that manner that Kasmin had been warned that, if he did not desist, vengeance, justice, would presently overtake him. A word to the wise was deemed sufficient. And, having dealt fairly, they would feel free, did he break faith, to deal with him according to their own code.

"I believe he's telling the truth," Critton declared excitedly. "And I suppose he came up here, really, to watch Kasmin—or, if Kasmin had failed to keep his promise and quit, or had broken faith, whatever it meant, then Pin H'sueh came here to kill him. And I suppose he did it."

But Mr. Pin denied that he had come here to watch Mr. Kasmin, or as an instrument of justice. It was almost a certainty, he admitted, that justice would have had to be administered out to Kasmin; men of his regrettable turn of mind gave promises intending to break them; they never reformed, and they scorned warnings. But Pin H'sueh had not known that Mr. Kasmin was coming here. He had worked faithfully for many years. He had been granted a vacation, had come here simply to visit his cousin.

Yes, he would be most happy not to leave Helena without first informing the police of his intentions, so that they might know where to write to him if need arose.

Back at the hotel again, they found that Sheriff Oliver had just arrived to see them. Joan Sargent was present, white-faced, but striving bravely to eat a little breakfast. Several other members of the party were gathered there. Leadley had been leafing through a late edition of a local paper, but now he tossed it aside. Hearle noted that it gave a long account of the case to date, dwelling particularly on the use that High Sing's laundry wagon had been put to. Nearly everyone concerned was pictured, including Jake Napoli, the Chicago gangster.

Hearle glanced inquiringly toward Critton. The prosecutor, meeting the glance, reddened a little but nodded.

"Yes, I gave the reporters a general outline of the story, leaving out the important things that we want kept quiet just now," he confessed. "They had to have something to print, and I thought it might as well be that as a garbled mess."

"I've been going over that roll of money we found on Napoli," the sheriff explained. "There was five hundred and fifty dollars in all, mostly in tens and twenties, and a lot of it was old money. So that made it a long job, and with the old bills, of course, it was impossible to discover anything.

"But there was one thing in our favor. There were four practically brand new bills, twenty dollar bills, and naturally they didn't have many finger prints on them. In fact, I found only three sets on two of them, and only one set on the other two. I gather that the one set of prints was that of a bank teller, who had opened a new package and paid them out. Being on the inside of the roll, between the other two new bills, those two had not been fingered at all, by anyone else.

"The other two bills," he went on slowly, "had been fingered a bit by Napoli himself—probably he was curious to see just how much money he had, and counted it. And those two bills also contained finger-prints of Mr. Sargent."

He stopped. Joan looked up suddenly, her eyes glittering with unshed tears. Leadley glanced at her with a softening of his own expression, then his jaw squared ominously.

"That implicates Napoli clearly enough in the crime, then," Critton cried. "I suspected him from the first. It proves clearly enough that he took the money that was in Sargent's pocket, and since he couldn't have done it after the affair at the jungle, he must have done it before. We're getting somewhere at last. Ready to go and talk to him now, Hearle?"

Hearle announced himself as ready. Leadley, with another glance toward Joan, also arose and took up his hat.

"I'm going with you and have a look at this fellow, too," he announced.

Jake Napoli had apparently regained his usual aplomb in the intervening hours, having reflected that there was really nothing against him, and he arose to greet them in his cell with an exaggerated show of courtesy. Lying in a corner of the cell, Hearle noted, was a copy of the same paper that

Leadley had been reading at the hotel.

This time, it was Hearle who asked the questions.

"You say that you came in on a freight train, some time Wednesday evening?" he asked.

"That's what I told you," Napoli smirked. "And if I told it to you, why you can sure tie to it as being correct."

"You never tell a lie, then?"

"Nope. Me and George Washington, we grew up in the same Sunday School class. We can't neither of us tell a lie."

Hearle passed this by.

"Then how was it," he asked, "that you came in on a freight, with a big roll of money in your pocket? I'd think that you'd have preferred to ride on the cushions. Or are you so used to rods that you feel away from home without them?"

"Sure, I'd have preferred the cushions, all right," Napoli grinned. "Only, you see, I'd run out of funds and had to wait till I reached me bankers again, as they wouldn't cash me check along the road without bein' identified. And that ain't always easy, you know, when you're travelin'."

"And as a rule, you would prefer not to be identified, eh? In that case, who are your bankers here?" Hearle's voice was as unruffled and patient as ever, though Critton looked angry at the taunting.

"I don't know who the gent was," Napoli confessed, still in that same bantering tone, "but I'd always heard that there was plenty gold around Helena, and my experience bears that out. I'll let you pass that on to the Commercial Club, if you

like. Course, it had been sort of shifted into bills
when I got hold of it, but then, them are just as
good with me. The way it was," he added, suddenly sober, "is that I hopped off the train down
near the tracks, and as I was walkin' along a path,
I saw a roll of bills layin' there. Maybe you think
I frisked somebody or used a blackjack to get them,
but I'm tellin' you the honest truth. I found them
layin' there, like some bloke had dropped them ac-
cidental. So of course I picked them up."

"You didn't say anything about them when we
questioned you before," Critton reminded him.

"Why should I?" Napoli countered. "You
didn't ask me. But when you did, I figured the
best way was to come clean, and I've done it."

"Oh, you've done it, eh? Been feeding us the
pure, lily-white facts, I suppose?" Critton's voice
was heavy with sarcasm. "Do you expect us to
believe that," he demanded, his voice suddenly a
roar of menace, "in view of the fact that we have
positively identified that roll of money, as belonging
to Richard Sargent, who was found murdered down
in the jungle? Do you think we're such fools as
that?"

Napoli's ruddy color deserted him, leaving his
face the color of old ashes. His little eyes stared
out, almost greenish in hue, burning with terror.
His fingers clenched and unclenched like claws seeking desperately to close on something substantial.
He passed his tongue nervously across his lips.

"You say—bo, what you givin' me?" he cried.
"You say you proved that money belongs to that
dead bloke?"

"Positive proof. And do you still think that

you can feed us any such a line as that, and get away with it? You aren't in Chicago any longer. Come clean, now. It will be better for you in the long run."

Napoli stared straight ahead for a long time while he considered the full possibilities of just what this meant. His jaunty aplomb of a few minutes before had quite deserted him, leaving him more like a cornered rat, desperate but not knowing how to fight. But finally he shook his head again, doggedly.

"I know how it looks," he admitted. "But it's God's truth I'm tellin' you, when I say that I found it. I never batted him over the head nor took it off him—never."

CHAPTER XV

Lon Leadley had stood in tense silence up to now, just inside the cell, a very much interested spectator, glaring down with a measure of rage and disgust at Napoli. Now, suddenly, he took two quick steps forward, and faced the gangster in a cold, deadly rage.

"You damned gutter rat," he growled hoarsely. "Don't lie now. If you're mixed up in this murder of Sargent, I'll see that you get the chair!"

Jake Napoli shrank back from the big man towering over him, but a startled light, as of recognition, was in his eyes now. For a long moment, while no one moved, he stood with his eyes fastened on Leadley's face. Then, nervously, his glance shifted to the crumpled newspaper, lying in a corner of his cell, darted to Hearle and Critton, back again to Leadley. A second time his tongue played across dry lips, a cunning light crept into his beady eyes. With it, was a venomous hatred like that of a rattlesnake about to strike.

"You ain't got nothin' on me," he snarled. "I'm givin' you the straight goods."

Hearle laid a restraining hand on Leadley's arm.

"Listen, Napoli," he said quietly. "We have discovered that Richard Sargent was not knocked over the head down in the jungle, by some passing tramp, but that he was murdered in his own room

127

in his hotel. Do you see the significance of your having his money in your pocket?"

"Oh, yeh, I see it, all right," Napoli grunted. "My tellin' that I found it sounds blamed funny, I know that, and prob'ly it won't do me no good. But I can't help it if luck gives me all the bad breaks, can I?"

But this time, Leadley's rage, which Hearle could see had been steadily mounting, overmastered him. The big man flung off the detective's arm impatiently, and spoke swiftly, in a voice quivering with passion.

"I can see that you're lying," he roared. "Anyone can see that you had a hand in murdering Sargent, and for that, whether it can be proved on you or not, you're going to sit in the electric chair. I can put you there, and I will. I remember you now. You're the dope runner that shot two policemen to death in Los Angeles last March, down at the pier. I happened to be in on that," he added, half-turning toward Hearle and Critton. "It was late at night, I had been working late and was driving around for a breath of air to clear my head and calm my nerves down so I could sleep.

"I heard shots, and saw this rat dash out of an alley, then crouch down and fire at two policemen who were after him. He killed both of them before I realized what was going on. When I did, I jumped out of my car and took after him. Caught him, too, and had a good look at his face. But he had a confederate who jumped me from behind, and between them they managed to give me a rap over the head and get away."

Hearle remembered the write-up of this event, which had been featured from coast to coast. If Leadley swore now that Napoli was the man so badly wanted on the coast for the double murder, no other evidence would be required to convict. As he said, he had the power to send Napoli to the chair. And Napoli too, had remembered and recognized him that was plain.

Leadley had swung back to Napoli.

"You got away then," he growled, "you dirty murderer. But I haven't forgotten that rat face of yours. If you hadn't murdered Sargent, I'd never have bothered to look at you, and you'd have gotten away again. But because you murdered him, you'll pay for it!"

He stopped, his jaw set in ugly lines. He was breathing heavily. The face of Napoli was truly that of a cornered rat, now that he was fairly caught, and knew it. But again Hearle detected that cunning, venemous gleam in his eyes, saw them shift momentarily to the newspaper and back again.

Astoundingly, Napoli shrugged. A sneer curved his thin lips. He seemed, all at once, to have regained complete control of himself. The taunting note was back in his voice again when he spoke.

"So you're goin' to pull the double-cross on me, and think you can save your own neck by watchin' me swing, eh?" he sneered. "That's just the way with your sort, every time—use a man as a tool, then when you get through with him, kick him down in the mud. But it don't go with me, not this time. I suppose you thought I was like a lot of them other fools in Chi—that I'd take

129

my medicine and never peep, eh? Well, I'm not doing it—not this boy. I'll swing, maybe, or sit on the hot seat, but I won't be alone. You'll be right there with me, waitin' your turn, and don't you forget it none."

He turned to the others, his voice rising suddenly to a shrill scream.

"You want the truth of what's been happenin' here, do you? Want to know who bumped off this Sargent guy? Well, you're goin' to get it, this time.

"He's the man that killed Sargent. Him, right there, the nice boy that's a movie hero to all the world and a murderin' sneak and yellow, double-crossin' skunk. Lon Leadley, as you call him. He's the man you've been lookin' for. Better put a pair of bracelets on him. He's dangerous."

Leadley had fallen back a step before the demoniac fury of the man. Now he stared at him, jaw sagging, eyes dilating. Napoli rushed on.

"You want the story, do you? Well, I'll tell it to you. You wonder where I got that roll of Sargent's—figured I was lyin' when I told you I picked it up; that that was too broad a one. Well, I was lyin', all right. I didn't pick it off of no path—but I did pick it up, picked it right out of Sargent's pocket after *he* had slugged him over the head. Oh yeh, I took it, all right. That was to be my share for helpin' with the job.

"I come in to town on the rods, like I said, without a red cent to me name, and not a bite to eat for two days. Down on my luck, and at the point where I had to do somethin'. I couldn't be choosey, not me. Only I come in Tuesday, not Wednesday

130

night. Bumped into Leadley on the street and put it up to him to give me a bit of money. Which he did, but not much——damn him. Wanted me broke, said he had a job for me pretty soon that'd pay good jack."

He paused, laughed hoarsely.

"Look at 'im," he taunted. "Ain't got a word to say now, has he? Goin' to see me cook, ain't he? Oh, yeh. And I suppose you're wonderin' why such a hero as him, that tried to catch me once, didn't turn me over to the police after he had caught me, seein' as I was wanted, or why the other day he didn't do the same thing, instead of givin' me a dollar? Well, I'll tell you that, too, pretty soon. Right now, I'm givin' you the low-down on this bumpin' off of Sargent, though I didn't have a thing to do with it, or know what was happenin' till after the guy'd been croaked.

"I didn't have any choice about whether I'd help out or not. Havin' caught me with the goods about them Los bulls that I croaked, Leadley had me where I had to do what he said, and when he told me he had a job for me, I done what I was told without askin' no questions. I helped him get that Chink's horse an' buggy away from the Chink kid, helped take it back in that alley, where the mud was about a foot deep, and we got plastered up right proper with it, doin' the job. But all I did then was stay out there, an' catch the body when he lowered it, then drive out to the jungles with him and help carry Sargent along that path and throw him off to the side. That's all I had to do about it. He done the dirty work himself,

131

and all I got for my share was what I found in
Sargent's pockets."

Leadley had listened, amazement and then anger
growing in his face at the tale. Now he straightened, laughed shortly, contemptuously.

"Of all the poppycock," he grunted. "Why, you
blasted rat, you——"

"Call me all the names you like," Napoli interrupted shrilly. "They won't do you no good.
I know enough to take you with me to hell, and
I'm sure going to do it. If you'd played square
with me, I'd of took what come along and kept my
mouth shut, but I ain't goin' to be no goat while
you play the hero. You gents are wonderin' what
it's all about," he went on rapidly, "and why he'd
want to bump off Sargent. Well, I can tell you
that, too."

Leadley shrugged contemptuously.

"Go ahead," he invited. "Let's see how good
an imagination you've got."

"I'll go ahead, all right, only it ain't imagination," Napoli responded vindictively. "That won't
be needed none. How do you suppose I really
got away from that big, hulking brute, down there
in Hollywood when I bumped them cops? Think
I could have done it, after he had hold of me, if
he hadn't wanted me to? He wanted the chance to
play the hero, but when he seen who he'd got hold
of, that he had one of his own tools, he still played
the hero and let me get away, too.

"Kasmin was out on the coast in a big dope-
peddlin' ring. But who do you figure was the
big shot in all this dope that's bein' peddled on the
coast? Kasmin? Not any, he wasn't. His head-

132

quarters was Chi, though he had a finger in it. The
man that was head—and is head—of the whole
business on the coast is Leadley there, the great
movie star. Made a nice cloak for his game, that
did. And I was one of his peddlers, for of
course he never done any of the work—not him.
Other men like me could do that, and run the
risk of gettin' shot or sent up to the big house for
it. All he did was keep back where it was safe
and take the profits—and believe me, he took plenty
for his share.

"There's them two—Leadley and Kasmin— you
saw 'em here together, didn't you? And there had
to be a reason, didn't there, for them birds bein'
together? And Sargent too? He was mixed up
in it, though just how, I don't know. But he was
another one in it, anyway. Tryin' to get the goods
on 'em, maybe, for the cops. Though the way it
looks to me, just three big leaders, and they got to
rowin' among themselves about the swag. Got to
the point where Leadley had to get rid of competi-
tion or else be got rid of, so he went ahead to do it.
First Kasmin, then Sargent.

"I don't know just where Sargent came in on
it," he went on thoughtfully. "But I figure he had
the job of bringin' in the dope from China and
so on. Sure did a lot of travelin' back and forth
from China to San Francisco and Los. Anyway,
I've told you how it happened. I know you've
got enough on me that I'll swing, but when a big
shot like Leadley thinks he'll just use me that
way, why, I ain't the sort of soft fool to keep my
mouth shut and let him get away with it. He

133

killed Sargent, and I helped him get rid of him afterward.''

He stopped; beady eyes darting restlessly about. They fastened for a moment on the crumpled newspaper in the corner, swept back to Leadley's face, paused briefly on Hearle's impassive countenance, jumped to Critton.

"You wanted the truth," he rasped. "Well, you got it. Tickled, ain't you? I wonder if you've got guts enough to arrest one of your own sort, now yuh got the goods on him? Ready enough to take a poor devil like me, but when it comes to a man with lots of swag and plenty of friends, that's somethin' else, ain't it? But you'll have to do it."

Critton stirred. His eyes snapped.

"You'll never find me hesitant when it comes to doing my duty," he grunted.

CHAPTER XVI

Silently, Hearle led the way out into the corridor. There the three men paused, confronting each other.

"You surely don't place any credence in what that yapping jackal has to say, do you?" Leadley demanded of Critton.

"As an officer of the law, I am compelled to pay some attention to it," Critton answered sharply. "Such charges cannot be disregarded."

"You mean that you intend to arrest me—on his word?"'

That's about the size of it, I guess," Critton agreed.

Leadley swung on Hearle.

"And you?" he asked. "Do you believe that I murdered Richard Sargent?"

"No," Hearle agreed bluntly. "I do not."

Critton stared at Hearle a moment, his jaw thrusting forward stubbornly.

"And accordingly, I suppose you would advise against arresting him?" he demanded.

"That would be my advice, yes—until this has been sifted a little further . Then, if evidence seems to justify it, that would be a different matter."

"There's been too much waiting, fooling around, all along in this case," Critton rasped. "You, with your authority, may of course do as you please,

135

but I have authority here to place any suspected man, to say nothing of a man charged with murder, under arrest. And I propose to use my authority as my judgment dictates."

"Certainly, my dear sir," Hearle agreed. "Still, even your judgment has not always proved to be infallible, even in this case. Would it not be well to wait a little while?"

"I'm not so sure about my judgment being all wrong in this case." Critton denied. "It seems to me that everything that I have suspected from the first, dovetails in very nicely. A row among the dope-runners explains everything. A motive was all that was lacking before, but that has been supplied. This explains all of Sargent's travels to the Far East and back, and so on. He was the only man on his feet in the room, when Kasmin was killed, while everyone was supposed to remain seated. Leadley and his man Gage no doubt connived at it, helped in the doing of it, perhaps, putting the lights out and so on.

"Then, after that was done, Leadley went ahead to rid himself of a dangerous rival in his business. The flashlight was found in Leadley's pocket. The—"

"You forget that Mr. Pinard also seemed to be implicated in this," Hearle suggested.

"I forget nothing. Doubtless he was and is implicated. Isn't he in, hand and glove, with Leadley here! There's a lot of things need sifting, and believe me, they're going to be sifted to the bottom, and some high-ups in Hollywood society are going to be shaken up."

"Then I'm under arrest?" Leadley inquired coldly.

"You're under arrest," retorted Critton promptly.

"In that case," said Leadley, whose temper had passed, leaving him calm and undisturbed, "I want to arrange to give bail at once."

"I doubt if you can get loose on bail at all," Critton retorted. "Murder is a serious charge, and I shall use my influence to see that you are not given bail."

"Use it, and be damned to you," Leadley retorted. He strode to the nearest phone, called briskly for a number. A minute later he turned back to them.

"Senator Ferguson will be up here in a few minutes," he informed Critton grimly. "See if your influence is greater than his."

The Senator arrived promptly. With him were Pinard, and Joan Sargent. The latter walked straight up to Leadley, and placed her hands on his shoulders.

"What is this dreadful thing I hear, Lon?" she asked him, an unmistakable note of tenderness in her voice.

"Mr. Critton has placed me under arrest for the murder of your father," Leadley retorted.

Joan swung about, her eyes blazing.

"Are you mad?" she cried at Critton, "to arrest him? Why he was one of Father's best friends. It is absurd."

"Absurd or not, he is charged with murder, and I intend to do my duty," Critton shrugged.

"I understand the court house is just across the street," Senator Ferguson interrupted. "Kindly lead the way over there, Mr. Critton, to the judge who has jurisdiction in this case. Come along, Leadley.

We will have this fixed up, so far as bail is concerned, very shortly."

The Senator's influence was far-reaching, and when he offered to stand surety personally for Leadley, no valid objection could be raised. Even Critton, apparently having reconsidered, raised no objections to the procedure.

"And now," said Eric Hearle, who had waited patiently while this was all attended to, "will you kindly come with me, Mr. Critton? I propose to help you do a little digging."

"With the greatest of pleasure," agreed Critton. Inwardly, he was reflecting that he had once been forced to apologize to this detective, and that, due to his impulsiveness, he might have to do it again before long. Of course, he had only done his sworn duty, in ordering the arrest of a man accused of murder. Still, he might have waited a little while, while Hearle continued his investigations. He had a disconcerting way of upsetting theories that seemed fool-proof.

Hearle's first step was to seek out Gage, in the hope that he might be able to afford a good alibi for his employer. Leadley had come up and joined Hearle when he had returned with Sargent the other night. But he had been with Hearle only a few minutes. After that, for some little time, his presence was unaccounted for. Also, there was only his word for it that he had come straight to Hearle's after returning. He might have gone first to Sargent's rooms with him. Also, Gage might have been implicated.

But Gage was able to offer no alibi. He had been on another floor of the hotel at the time, he explained, attending to some small duties. Hence, he could furnish no alibi either for Leadley or himself.

"Looks darned suspicious to me, any way you take it," Critton declared, his confidence beginning to rise again. "Unless someone can establish an alibi, it could all have been done in just the way it was. And then there was Pinard mixed up in it, too."

"Those who are guilty always have alibis prepared," Hearle pointed out. "The innocent do not think of such things."

Hearle continued patiently his effort to discover whether any member of the party, or any one around the hotel, could afford the proof as to Leadley's presence at that hour. Leadley himself presently returned, to declare that he had been alone in his own rooms.

"Will you kindly get hold of the officer who picked Napoli up, and ask him to report up at the jail?" requested Hearle. "I think that we will be able to clear this little matter up before the time for the funeral, this afternoon. It would appear scarcely seemly for the man charged with murder to attend the funeral of his victim, but on the other hand, it would be unseemly for a host to fail to attend the funeral of his friend and guest."

Critton agreed. A quarter of an hour later they returned to the county jail. The officer waited, expectantly, but Hearle merely led the way again to Napoli's cell, and turned to Napoli himself.

"We merely wish to clear up one or two little points," Hearle explained. "You said first, I believe, that you came in on a freight train, and arrived in Helena sometime during the forepart of Wednesday night. Am I correct?"

"That's what I said, yeh," Napoli agreed. "And it's correct enough, except that I come in before then, on Tuesday, as I told you later."

"Yes. You were arrested in the general round-up of suspicious characters on Thursday forenoon, by this officer, were you not?"

"Yeh. Guess I was."

Hearle turned to the officer.

"Just where did you find him?"

"He was skulkin' in a little alley, up in China-town, then. I thought he looked suspicious and took him in."

"I see. And do you still contend, Napoli, that when you came to Helena, at whatever time it was, that you were broke, riding the rods?"

"That's true enough."

"Did you have any possessions with you, of any sort—anything that might have been turned into money?"

"Not a blamed thing. I had just the clothes I've got on now."

"The same clothes? They look rather as though they had seen some hard service."

"They sure have, too, and that's no joke."

"H'm. As I understand it, you presently had the good fortune to run into Mr. Leadley, who recognized you, loaned you a small sum of money, and said that he would have a job for you later on?"

"That's the straight of it, I reckon."

"He didn't give you much money?"

"You're darn right he didn't. Just enough to get a couple of meals on."

"You found no other opportunity for earning money—by working, begging, or robbing?"

"No. I figured if he had somethin' good comin' up, I'd better not get mixed up in anything that might interfere. He wouldn't have liked that."

"And then, when you did help him, you aided him in stealing the horse and buggy from the Chinese boy?"

"Yep, I helped him do that."

"Where did you get the outfit?"

"Oh, back up in an alley in Chinktown."

"And you rapped the boy over the head?"

"No, Leadley did that himself."

"What happened after that?"

"Well, we drove around by back streets till we could get to that alley, and since it was so blame narrow, all closed at one end, we had to unhitch the horse an' back the buggy in by hand. Then, while I hitched the horse up again, Leadley went back in the hotel and pretty soon he lowered the body to me."

"I see. The alley was muddy, wasn't it?"

"Muddier'n hell, yeh."

"You contrived to keep in the buggy all the time, though, I suppose?"

"Then yuh sure suppose wrong. I had to splash around in all the sticky—"

Napoli stopped suddenly, a startled look in his eyes, glanced down at his feet. Hearle followed the glance, smiled.

"I suppose his shoes were badly covered with mud when you picked him up the next morning, weren't they, officer?"

141

"They wasn't muddy at all, unless it was on the soles a little," the officer declared.

"Were his shoes wet, then?"

"Not a bit."

"Strange. Because they show no sign of having been scraped dry of a great deal of mud. In fact, I would say that they had never had much mud on them. If they had been in a lot of mud, it would have been necessary, to get them to their present state, to wash them very thoroughly, and naturally, they would still have been rather wet the next morning, or otherwise show some traces of being either cleaned or in that deep mud."

He stooped, suddenly, and before Napoli could understand his intention or protest, had jerked off the left shoe and held it up for all to see.

"Observe it," he invited Critton. "First of all, it's a low oxford, rather the worse for wear. But if he had tramped around in that alley mud, six inches deep at the least, it would have gone well over the tops of these shoes, have soaked down inside. These linings have never been stained with mud. And although he has admitted that these were the shoes he came to town with, we'll stop any further alibi by pointing out that his left foot is rather twisted—accordingly, an ordinary shoe would not fit it at all. He has to have shoes made to order, and inside here is the name of the maker, in Chicago. Pah," he tossed the shoe back to Napoli with a gesture of disgust.

"You're a clumsy liar, Napoli. You told the truth in the first place, that you found the roll of money. Sargent's murderers, rather than keep it, because it might be used as possible evidence against

142

them, threw it away down there in the jungle, since they wanted to further the idea of robbery and murder, and it wouldn't do to leave it on him. You found it.

"And then, today, when Leadley recognized you for the murderer that was wanted back in Los Angeles, you realized that the game was up. No matter what happened, it was the chair for you. But you're a crafty, treacherous devil, and you had just been reading an account of all that had happened in this case, in the paper. You had a lot of photos and names to study, so that you recognized Leadley all right when you saw him, and it occurred to you that you'd cause him some trouble, might even be able to cause him a lot, by making up that story. That would give you some measure of revenge for his identification of you, which will send you to the chair. But you forgot about your shoes when you were making up that story about the muddy alley."

At first, Napoli had listened with an expression of disgust and faint admiration on his face. But by now he had regained most of his aplomb again. He seemed to enjoy the expression on Critton's face.

"You've got the right of it," he admitted to Hearle. "But I did cause him some trouble, I guess, and it'll be in all the papers, before this denial comes out, the big movie hero arrested for murder and bein' the head of a dope ring. Oh, yeh, I guess I've nothin' to kick about. And then I like to see men like you squirm," he added to Critton. "And it was sure easy to fool you. You fell for the whole yarn."

143

"I suppose that you'll order the release of Leadley now?" Hearle suggested, when they were out in the corridor again.

Critton turned a tortured face to the detective.

"Of course," he agreed. "What kind of an ass must you think me, Mr. Hearle? And Leadley—I'll apologize, but—what a blundering fool! From here on, Hearle, this case is entirely in your hands."

CHAPTER XVII

The last services had been conducted for Richard Sargent. Hearle, about to pick his way back to a car for the return to the city, noted the local pastor, who had conducted the services, in animated conversation with Pinard. Having finished his task, the minister had relaxed, was smiling, genial. Pinard beckoned to Hearle.

"I would like to have you meet Mr. Overton," he explained. "He was formerly pastor of a church down in Los Angeles, before coming up here a couple of years ago, and we became very well acquainted in those days."

"I'm certainly glad to know you, Mr. Hearle," the minister replied sincerely. "Mr. Pinard has been telling me what excellent work you're doing on this case. It has been a great pleasure for me to see Mr. Pinard again. We used to have some great times together down in California." He smiled reminiscently. "I'm afraid, however, that he considers me rather a poor guide to the country around here.

"Take the other evening, for instance—Wednesday evening, I think it was. I had suggested that a very pretty view of the city could be obtained at night from up on Mount Helena, and so Pinard insisted on going through with a hike we had planned, even though the rain turned to a regular downpour just as we were about to start. But we had a most enjoyable time of it, at that, climbing in the dark, with only a flashlight, slipping and sliding around in the mud."

"It must have been pleasant," Hearle agreed politely. "Did you enjoy the trip, Pinard?"

Pinard grinned but made no comment.

"He's really too polite to express his real feelings, I guess," Mr. Overton commented. "And then he was rather peeved at the start of the trip. We had discovered an old laundry wagon that one of the Chinese uses, and Pinard seemed to be greatly struck with its appearance.

" 'That's a genuine antique,' he exclaimed. 'The real, authentic west is in it. I'd like to get hold of it. It could be used very effectively in a picture that Leadley plays the lead in, as soon as we get back.'

"And so he stopped the boy who was driving it, and the boy told him to go jump in the lake." The minister chuckled. "Since we were, more or less, in the lake already, it really sort of spoiled our trip for Pinard, I guess."

Presently they parted. Pinard accompanied Hearle back to a car, turning for one last look toward the spot where Richard Sargent rested. Quite unaffectedly he removed his hat as he gazed.

"There was a man," he said simply. "A gentleman of the old school. I was proud to call him friend. He had a code of honor as undeviating as the best traditions of the old South—and being from Virginia myself, I know whereof I speak. Ordinary considerations were never enough with him. Everything had to square up with his strict sense of justice before he was satisfied.

"I'm thinking, chiefly," Pinard went on, "of a business deal that we entered into several years ago. I had gotten wind of an old, supposedly worked-out gold mine in California. It seemed to me that it might be made to pay by the use of modern machinery. Since I couldn't swing it myself in those days, I put it up to Dick. He never bothered to investigate it at all, just took my word for it and put up half the money necessary—a hundred thousand dollars.

"Well, we sunk the whole two hundred thousand, and seemed no nearer to gold than we had been before. We hadn't got a dollar back out of it. I investigated it again, and it looked hopeless to me. I suggested pocketing our losses and forgetting it. I was about broke then, though, and kind of down-hearted. Sargent knew how my affairs were.

"So he insisted on paying me back what I had put in, and declared that he wanted to own the full interest, anyway. Then he went ahead and put in a lot more money. And he struck the gold, too, that we thought was there. Since then, that mine has paid back nearly three million dollars."

Pinard paused, and stared ahead unseeingly.

"That was rather a tough break for you," Hearle commented sympathetically.

Pinard's head came up with a jerk.

"Tough for me?" He laughed, harshly. "Nothing of the kind. For though I had no shadow of a claim to it then, Richard Sargent was the sort of a man who, as I have just told you, had a strict code of honor. He insisted that half of the mine belonged to me, forced me to pay him back that

hundred thousand, despite all that I could say—
he claimed that he couldn't be at ease with his own
conscience if he cheated me—and gave me back
my half-interest.

"Even then, on the day that I paid him back
the hundred thousand, I received exactly the same
amount back as my share of the profits to date.
Since then, I've had a half of the total. That's
the kind of man Richard Sargent was, and, leaving him back there, I felt that I had to say it, to
someone. And, since I know that you have had
suspicions of him, in this first murder, I felt that
you were the man to say it to."

He sat back, relapsed into silence for the rest of
the drive. Hearle too, was silent. The case against
Pinard had collapsed. Here was an alibi that could
not well be doubted. It had not been manufac-
tured, Hearle was positive of that. The minister
would be no party to trickery.

And yet the fact remained that both John Kasmin and Richard Sargent had been murdered, the
crimes being committed with a fiendish ingenuity.
Someone was guilty, and must be made to pay. It
merely meant, Hearle reflected with a little sigh,
that he must begin once more, and build a new
structure that would stand more firmly.

Leadley was planning to go out to his ranch on
the Dearborn the next day, which was Saturday,
and take his guests with him. The two murders
had put a decided damper on the vacation spirit,
but those who remained, including Joan Sargent
herself, agreed that the original program might as
well be carried through, even though it had been

somewhat delayed. Hearle, since the party would still be sticking together, had no objections.

He did recall one social engagement for this last evening before departure from town, however. He had promised High Sing to come and partake of some real Chinese noodles before he left town. So, as the shadows began to lengthen, he picked his way up through Chinatown until he came to the house of High Sing, crouching back against the hill.

"I really should have let you know in advance," Hearle apologized. "But I didn't know when I could come, and I couldn't phone you, as I discovered, so I came to tell you that it was all right anyway. I will be glad to have you come as my guest to one of the regular noodle parlors."

High Sing, however, had a better idea.

"We go regular noodle parlor, all right," he agreed. "But you go as my guest, and my friend, he fix us the regular Chinese noodles. He better cook than me, anyway. Charley," raising his voice, and when the boy appeared, his grandfather dispatched him ahead at top speed with the proper instructions to the restaurant proprietor. Then, more leisurely, Hearle and High Sing followed together through the pleasant evening, redolent with the scents of springtime.

An occasional car droned by along the streets, but Chinatown was for the most part quiet and peaceful as they came to the noodle parlor of Guei Shan, unprepossessing as to exterior but filled with closely curtained booths within. Past these, however, the proprietor led them, having greeted them ceremoniously at the door, and so to a little private room

149

in the rear. There, with assurances that the feast would presently be ready, he left them.

They talked for a few minutes, Hearle's host dwelling entertainingly on early days in Helena. He had often seen Colonel Sanders, though the Vigilante days were past when he had arrived at the gold camp. Names famous the country over flowed smoothly from his lips. He had seen one or two disastrous fires sweep the early wooden mining camp, had watched the new city gradually rise up from the ashes of the old.

The noodles arrived, and they fell silent. High Sing handled the chop sticks dextrously, but Hearle found it sufficient of a puzzle to manipulate the noodles with a fork. The food, though, he conceded, was excellent—far different from the noodles he had been accustomed to in the past. High Sing beamed approval.

Gradually, Hearle became aware of two other voices, somewhere beyond them, in a curtained booth of the restaurant—quietly modulated voices, speaking in a softly flowing, yet penetrating speech. Hearle listened for a few minutes, his interest quickening. Then he turned to his host.

"Are those two men speaking Chinese?" he asked. High Sing nodded.

"Chinese, yes," he agreed. "But not the language as I know it—not the dialect of the South."

"You mean—they are speaking Mandarin?"

"I think that is it, yes."

Hearle's eyes glittered. He leaned forward.

"It sounds to me as though they were both speaking it with equal fluency. Is that your opinion?"

150

"It sound so, yes. Both talk fast—like native."

"Tell me, High Sing, would it be possible for a foreigner—say, an American, or even a Japanese, to pick up the Chinese language and speak it as smoothly as they are doing?"

High Sing shook his head vigorously.

"No could be done. Chinese, it very difficult language for foreigner. Even Chinaman, scholar, no can talk other dialect perfectly. May talk it good, yes—but native can tell it not his mother tongue. You know, even Englishman can not talk United States the way you do."

Hearle nodded agreement.

"And do you know the speakers?" he asked.

High Sing cocked his head on one side a moment, listening. His was the air of a judge.

"One, he Pin H'sueh, cousin of Lee Hung," he nodded. "But other—he stranger to me. Both Chinamen, though."

Hearle did not pursue the subject. He was pleased with High Sing's corroboration, for he had himself decided that one of the voices was that of Pin H'sueh, who had at last found someone who could talk to him in his own tongue. And the other voice, which High Sing also declared to be that of a Chinaman, was the voice of Yamamoto—Yamamoto, the servant of Louis Jouralmon. Yamamoto claimed to be a Japanese, and he had taken a Japanese name. He spoke the language of the Mandarins of China. Accordingly, he practiced a deception in regard to his name and nationality. Why?

And again, why should Pin H'sueh and Yamamoto be in conversation together? Of course, if

151

both were natives of the north of China, speaking a common language, it was, in a way, quite natural, especially in a city where no one else could speak their native tongue. Yet, since Yamamoto evidently wished to keep his nationality secret, there was something strange about it. And why should he happen to be acquainted with Pin H'sueh, how come to reveal his secret to him?

CHAPTER XVIII

For a few minutes, Hearle and his host ate in comparative silence. The other voices had also died down to a low and infrequent murmur, only faintly audible now and again. Then there came stealing, faintly, an elusive perfume to the nostrils of Hearle. At first he took no note of it, since it was so faint as to be almost imperceptible, a silver thread upon the air. Then some quality of it called up recollection in his memory, stored there from years ago in a dim spot in New York City. He turned to stare about; smiled at High Sing.

"Some one," he remarked quietly, "smokes opium."

High Sing nodded placidly.

"So it would seem," he agreed.

"Can you discover for me who it is?" Hearle asked. "If it is either of our Mandarin friends, I am interested. If not—" he spread his hands expressively.

High Sing nodded. He arose on padded slippers with the quietness of a stalking cat, slipped like a shadow out of the doorway and was gone. Two minutes, three, while that faint perfume, so oddly intangible, strayed elusively like a forgotten melody upon the air. Then he was back again.

"Pin H'sueh, he smoke," he reported. "His com-

153

panion, he glare at him and mutter angrily, disdain
the pipe. But Pin H'sueh smoke anyway."

"And yet Pin H'sueh would have us to believe
that he fights to destroy opium, that he is a man
who would never touch it himself," Hearle commented. "It may be, of course, that he fights the
poppy while being himself a slave to it—but I
doubt that. It doesn't seem logical."

"He liar if he say so," declared High Sing
promptly. "Slave to poppy love its master, never
fight it. I have seen too much, many, many
years."

"I'm inclined to think you're right," Hearle
agreed. "In which case, all that Pin H'sueh has
told us is likely for the purpose of throwing mud
in our eyes."

Having praised the noodles fittingly, he returned
with the old man to High Sing's house, silently
for most of the way. At the door, however, he
made a request.

"If it is not too much trouble, could your grandson, Charley, come with me for a little while now?
I should like him as a guide about the town."

High Sing readily agreed, and called the boy.
And presently the two stopped at the home of Lee
Hung. Lee Hung himself greeted thm ceremoniously. He regretted, he explained, that his cousin,
Pin H'sueh, whom Hearle had no doubt called to
see, was not at the moment present. He had gone,
he explained, to see a movie that evening.

Hearle reflected that Pin H'sueh's movie was no
doubt composed of fantastic fables in the land of
paradise, but he made no comment.

"Pin H'sueh is fond of movies, then?" he asked.

"Yes," Lee Hung agreed, as though slightly puzzled. "He go every night or so, take one, two, in. Flicker of the moving figures hold great fascination, he aver."

"But you do not care for the movies, eh, Lee Hung? You are an old man, steeped in the wisdom of the years, and are above such petty frivolties?"

Lee Hung smiled, shook his head.

"The wise man is ever a seeker after knowledge," he quoted, "and he knows not in what strange places it may be found. Pin H'sueh, he still young man. Me, I old man now, I like stay home nights, sleep much. My company tiresome for young man, I suppose."

"He leaves you alone every night, then?" Hearle appeared to be shocked at this breach of hospitality.

Lee Hung felt called upon to defend his guest.

"He stay home last night," he stated, with a shrill cackle of laughter. "We have long talk on paper, he see me nod in chair. Laugh. Say he not bother me evenings again."

"Oh, well, if you had a good sleep the night before—"

Lee Hung grinned guiltily.

"Would have had," he agreed. "Only I get absent-minded, lock my door. When Pin H'sueh come, he have to wake me up to open door to get in."

"That was an awfully rainy night, I remember. He must have hated to be kept standing out in the rain."

"Oh, it stop raining before he come home. He

155

under cover anyway, I guess. His shoes dry and nice. Pin H'sueh, he take care of himself."

Regretting that Pin H'sueh was not there, but adding that it was of no importance, Hearle and the boy took their leave. Hearle was puzzled. Pin H'sueh had been out late that night, which coincided with the theory he had formed. But Lee Hung declared that his cousin had returned dry shod, which immediately spoiled that theory.

"Pin H'sueh, he take care of himself!"

Hearle paused, staring ahead at a patch of darkness as though he expected to see something unusual emerge from it. Suddenly he swung on the boy.

"Charley, is there any kind of a shop kept here by some old Chinaman—a second hand store, or a cobbler's shop, or something like that?"

"Yat Sen keeps such a place," Charley replied promptly. "He does some work on shoes, and keeps sort of a junk shop, too."

"Take me there, will you?"

Charley led the way, by devious paths, for a couple of blocks, stopped before a house which stood dark and silent now.

"I reckon he's asleep now," Charley grinned. "But I'll get him up."

He moved around to a window, stood on tiptoe and rapped sharply, then went back to the door and repeated the summons. Presently a light glowed somewhere within, quite obviously a candle, a bolt rattled in the door, and Yat Sen stood there, like a dried apple, candle held high, peering out.

"All time be waked up," he complained querulously. "No can sleep any more. What you want, Charley?"

Charley explained, and a little of Yat Sen's ill-humor vanished as he saw Hearle. He stood aside, and invited them to enter.

Hearle glanced curiously about at the jumble of stuff, most of which Charley had aptly described as junk. Noting a little bronze Buddha, he inquired the price and purchased it, to the quite apparent gratification of Yat Sen. Then, turning as if to depart, Hearle paused.

"I'm sorry to have disturbed you at this hour," he explained, "but I'm leaving town in the morning. You said something about being bothered all the time lately. I trust it doesn't happen very often?"

"Not bad," Yat Sen explained, affably now. "Two nights ago, man come in here, shoes awfully muddy. He Chinaman, but no can understand him very well. Think shoes spoiled, but they only need clean. Anyway, he insist on buy pair of old shoes I have, wear them. Leave others for me to clean."

"Well, I'm sorry that I had to disturb you," Hearle repeated, and amid assurances that it was quite all right, took his departure. He thanked Charley High and sent him home, then went slowly back to his own hotel. At last the tangle seemed to be straightening out a little. There could be no question now that Pin H'sueh was implicated in the murders, at least in the second one, of Richard Sargent. There was little less question that Yamamoto was implicated with him. It all worked out nicely—up to a certain point. Beyond that were false trails still, stumbling-blocks which seemed hard to remove. As he walked, he ran the whole

thing over in his mind, from the beginning. The
dinner at which John Kasmin had been a guest,
had been fearful of having the lights turned out—
or of having his picture taken. Which?

The camera had been brought in by Gage, set
up, moved, the lights turned out. Then stalking
tragedy. The talking at first; silence; little hushed,
significant noises, among them the low, steady
clicking hum of the automatic camera, the questions
of Leadley, Gage's replies; the lights on again; and
John Kasmin dead in his chair.

"The camera," Hearle muttered to himself.
"And tonight, opium! Yes, I believe we're beginning to get somewhere at last."

The other members of the party were all asleep
when he returned to the hotel, so Hearle, mindful
of the hard day ahead, sought his own rest. Morning found him ready to continue on the trail that
he had unearthed the evening before. He had, as
he reminded himself, a very nice theory. But so
far as proof was concerned, he was no further along
than when he had started. And in a court of law,
proof was the only thing that counted.

Yamamoto hurried by, busily intent on some
errand. Hearle called to him.

"Could you spare me just a few minutes soon,
Yamamoto? I want to ask you something."

Yamamoto smiled politely, and set down what
he was carrying.

"I am most happy to help now if I can," he
agreed.

The shirt that Yamamoto was wearing was of
an unobtrusive but rather unusual pattern, Hearle
noted. He remembered that it was the same shirt

158

that Yamamoto had worn on Tuesday evening—
or else one exactly like it. Probably it had been
laundered in the meantime, since this was Saturday,
and would be the same shirt. But Yamamoto's
sober black coat was buttoned over it. Hearle's
fingers closed on a little white button in his own
coat pocket.

"I've always been curious about this art of jiu-
jitsu, that is practised in Japan," he explained.
"And I was wondering if you would be so good as
to show me one or two of the holds used." He
proceeded to remove his own coat, placing it over
the back of a chair, and stood revealed in his shirt
sleeves. The button that Gage had picked off the
floor on that first fatal night was hidden in his
fingers.

Yamamoto smiled again, removed his own coat,
and turned to face Hearle. The detective's eyes
swept sharply over his shirt front. Every button
was neatly in place, all of a size. But one, Hearle
noted, was sewed on with criss-cross thread—it
would have been a button with four holes. The
other buttons did not have that criss-cross thread.
They were buttons with only two holes, the ones
that had come with the shirt. The button in
Hearle's hand was a two-hole button!

Suddenly, without warning, Yamamoto had
leaped forward, still smiling. It was as though a
hurricane had struck him. So quickly that it left
him bewildered, Hearle found himself off his feet,
on his back on the floor; then, almost in the same
dexterous motion, he had been lifted up again, and
Yamamoto was solicitously brushing off a fleck of
dust.

159

"Excuse the quickness," he said. "But I show you by the demonstration how it works. Shall I show you now, slow? Or another time?"

"Another time will do, thank you, Yamamoto," Hearle replied, putting on his coat. Inwardly he was cursing himself for his folly in giving Yamamoto that excuse for the attack. It had all been so bewilderingly swift—but in those few moments, the button had somehow been wrested from his fingers, had disappeared out the open window, to fall in the street below. As he glanced toward the street, Hearle saw a big sprinkling wagon passing, its flood of water sweeping every small object before it, into the recesses of the gutters.

CHAPTER XIX

Hearle took up his coat, endeavoring to conceal his chagrin. That an old hand like himself should be made such a fool of by Yamamoto! The only real piece of evidence that they had, to be so swiftly lost at the critical moment. Yamamoto had seen or guessed what his purpose was, and had acted promptly. He was a dangerous antagonist, Hearle realized, and even now he was politely helping Hearle on with his coat. But Hearle's own face was smiling now.

"I'm very much obliged for the demonstration, Yamamoto," he said, significantly. "I'll be sure to remember it. The food at Guei Shan's is excellent, isn't it?"

For just a moment, a startled flicker showed in Yamamoto's eyes. Hearle added another dart to the wound.

"The man who smokes opium is apt to be loose-tongued!"

Again that flicker, with something akin to panic back of it. Then Yamamoto's face was a polite mask of interest again. But there was no doubt that he understood. Moreover, he could have no way of knowing how much the detective knew. Had Pin H'sueh, under the influence of the opium, been induced to talk? And if so, how much had he told?

161

Hearle said no more, but dismissed Yamamoto about his own duties. Everyone was excitedly busy now, the cars already waiting in the street below, to take them out to Leadley's ranch on the Dearborn. Two girls appeared, their heads close together.

"Good morning, Margaret, and Elinor," Hearle greeted them politely. "A lovely day for our trip, isn't it?"

The two girls turned at the greeting, and Hearle noted disconcertedly that one of the girls was not Margaret Ferguson, but Joan Sargent. He shook his head as though to clear away a web. He was certainly getting careless lately.

"My mistake," he apolwogized. "But from be-hind, with those helmet hats pulled to hide your hair, you do look remarkably alike."

"I think that is a desirable achievement," Eli-nor laughed. "To look like Joan here is a high compliment."

Hearle shook his head with a rueful smile and passed on. Just at the present moment, while not appearing to do so, he wished to keep an eye on the movements of Yamamoto.

A glance showed him that Jouralmon was al-ready waiting down in one of the cars, a big, open touring car. Hearle raised his eyebrows slightly at this as he went up to the car, and Lead-ley, catching the look, explained.

"About twenty miles from here, we enter the Prickly Pear canyon," he said. "It's nearly twenty miles long, a deep, narrow gorge, full of cliffs and pine trees. One of the finest bits of scenery in the state, or in the world, for that matter. And to

get a good view of it an open car is really a necessity."

"I was wondering about the open cars myself,"
Jouralmon commented. "But they will be very
pleasant on such a day as this. How soon do we
start now, Leadley?"

"Within fifteen or twenty minutes, I hope.
Everybody should be ready by then."

Yamamoto descended from the hotel, carrying a
couple of bags, which he proceeded to stow away.
Then he moved over to Jouralmon and, with
scarcely a glance at anyone else, spoke swiftly, low-
toned, in what sounded a veritable jumble of
words. He was speaking either in Chinese or
Japanese.

Jouralmon listened, his face a careless mask during the recital—rather too much so, Hearle decided.
At the conclusion he smiled.

'So. Oh, well, that will be all right—don't
worry about it any.' But, Yamamoto, I want you
to go up to that little store on Broadway and get
a package that I bought there yesterday—I meant to
remind you before, but you'll still have time, by
hurrying. It's—" he spoke swiftly, a sentence or
so in the same language that Yamamoto had used.

"Be sure and don't make any mistake in this
now," he ended. "It's important."

"I will make no mistake," Yamamoto agreed, and
re-entered the hotel. A minute later he came out
and hurried up the street.

Jouralmon stood up in the car, fumbled in his
pockets, yawned.

"I think I'll just step into a cigar store and get

163

me a package of cigarettes while I'm waiting," he decided.

He walked leisurely down the street a few doors, disappeared through one. Hearle had sauntered off, across the street. Now he moved swiftly, circling a short block up the hill, came, a minute later, to a rear door of the same cigar store, fronting on another and less busy street. He moved in here, glanced swiftly around the store. Jouralmon was nowhere to be seen, but the door to a small telephone booth was closed.

Hearle lost himself in contemplation of an ancient wooden Indian, which had probably, years agone, stood in front of the store, but had for long years been relegated to the musty recesses of the store. From this point he was shut off from view of the phone booth, while able to watch it quite clearly.

A moment later, Jouralmon came out, paused at the counter to thank the proprietor and make his purchase, sauntered on out to the street. Hearle stepped swiftly into the booth.

"Operator," he called. Then: "Can you please tell me what number the last speaker just called? I am Eric Hearle, detective in charge of the investigation of the murders of Kasmin and Sargent. The county attorney's office will vouch for me."

The operator was soon satisfied, and answered pleasantly.

"You mean the Chinaman that just called up?" she demanded. "He called M729L."

"Thank you," Hearle replied, and hung up. He leafed through the phone book which hung there, turning first to the name of Lee Hung. The number opposite it was M729L.

Hearle also made a small purchase, commented admiringly on the wooden Indian, and went out again at the back door. Presently from an opposite direction, he returned to the car, where Jouralmon was again seated.

By this time everyone was ready. Yamamoto, however, had not yet returned. Leadley was clearly impatient to be off. Jouralmon glanced at his watch.

"We won't wait any longer for him," he declared. He beckoned to a bell boy, who bustled up. Jouralmon pressed a bill into his hand.

"When my servant, Yamamoto—you know him when you see him—returns, tell him that we've gone on," he instructed. "Tell him to hire a car to bring him out to Mr. Leadley's ranch on the Dearborn."

"Yes sir," the boy agreed. "I'll tell him."

"No need of waiting," Jouralmon declared. "He may have had trouble in finding the place, or the package might not be ready. He can come afterward just as well."

So, several days behind schedule, the party rolled away toward the Dearborn. It was, save for the Prickly Pear canyon, a swift, pleasant ride. The canyon itself was necessarily slow, due to the winding, narrow roads, but this, as everyone agreed, was only proper, for the scenery was worth a long look. Slightly before midday they reached the ranch itself, squatting up in the foothills of the main range of the Rockies, wooded with jack pine and spruce to a considerable extent. One big, rambling log house, with several smaller cabins, sprawled invitingly at the foot of a hill, a trout stream rambled by less than a quarter of a mile in front of the door. Off to one side was a big barn and an old corral.

"Since this is a dude ranch we have to keep up the old time fixtures," Leadley explained. "Cowboys of the old school, cattle, the barns and corrals, everything. Not many of the boys are here right now, however. They're on an upper range, and will drift down here about the time that the regular dude season begins—about the time that we leave."

"I imagine that you can do that sort of thing pretty well yourself, Leadley," the Senator commented.

"Well, I used to do the real thing, for a fact," Leadley admitted. "Many's the day I've ridden all day behind a big herd, sweated in the branding pen, worked in the loading chutes in the stockyards—there's a lot of the old west still lives, once you get back away from the cities and railroads a little. About tomorrow, we'll take pack horses and work back up in the mountains several miles, and then you'll see some of the real, primeval country. We'll spend a few days back up there. It can't be reached except on foot or horseback."

They alighted from the cars, and most of the guests went up to the house, where everything was in readiness. There would be no "paying guests" until after they had left. Leadley, noting Hearle's quick-eyed interest, and the evident desire of the others to rest up first, suggested a brief stroll of inspection. Hearle accepted eagerly.

Together they looked at the corrals. Leadley

166

explaining the operation of the dehorning chute, indicating a few blackened rocks where a fire had been kindled for heating the branding iron, moved on into the cool recesses of the big barn, one side of which was filled to the roof with hay. From somewhere came a small, regular, puzzling sound. Leadley, noting Hearle's look, grinned.

"That will be Gibney," he explained. "Practising his hobby. Come quietly and look."

He led the way to a room at one end of the barn, indicated a convenient knot hole. Peering through this, Hearle beheld a man, rather slight in build, of perhaps fifty years of age. His hair was gray, his face deeply seamed and lined, though his blue eyes were very bright. He was dressed, just now, in high boots and khaki trousers, with a blue denim shirt open at the neck. Yet the trousers were clean and carefully pressed, the boots highly polished, neatness predominating. His arms moved with a regular, rhythmic motion, and Hearle was struck by the smooth play of powerful muscles under the shirt sleeve.

But that which most caught his eye was not the man himself, unusual a character as he was, but what he was about. At the far end of the room he had nailed up a thick square of pine board, about two feet in diameter. Across this were drawn small circles, not above two inches in size, and each one numbered. Sticking in each of the dozen circles now was a long, evil-bladed bowie knife, the points buried for perhaps two inches in the wood.

Even as they watched, the little man stepped across to the knives, jerked each one swiftly out, then went back to his former position, some dozen

167

feet away. With swift, unerring skill, he again hurled each knife, and they sped true to the mark, one, two, three, and so on up to twelve, till the last blade hung quivering, its point buried deep in the board.

They tiptoed away.

"That's Gibney," Leadley explained. "He hates to show off, so we won't let on that we saw it. Its his hobby—picked it up somewhere in the East, he explains it—Sumatra, China or somewhere. A strange character, Gibney. He has been a gentleman, that's plain enough, and has delved into more unlikely places over the face of the earth than you could mention in five minutes of steady talking. He was rather down on his luck, so I hired him as head man up here. He's a crackerjack at anything he undertakes."

Talking now, naturally, they approached the room again, and Gibney came out to meet them. Leadley introduced him, and again Hearle was impressed by the grip of steel fingers. Together then, they strolled toward the house, and there, not as an employee but as a social equal, Leadley proceeded to introduce Gibney to his guests.

Despite his position and rough clothes, Gibney was in no way embarrassed. Hearle saw that what Leadley had said was true. The man was a gentleman, accustomed to any society. He could have sat down with equal grace and unconcern to dine with the King of England or with the humblest, most illiterate cockney of London's squalor, and either of them would have felt at home with him in turn—no condescension toward the cockney, no fawning or sense of inferiority toward the king.

168

Mrs. Reid was frankly pleased with him, regarding him somewhat in the light of an unusual specimen. A light leaped to the Senator's eyes which told that he had met a kindred spirit. Jouralmon was the last to be introduced. Gibney's eyes brightened a trifle, recognition leaped to them, coupled with a quizzical look. But Jouralmon's face was blank.

"Hello—Jouralmon," Gibney said, with a scarcely noticeable pause before speaking the name. "Don't remember me, eh? Good many years since we met, in an odd corner of the globe, isn't it? A big world, and yet not so big."

"I'm afraid that you have the advantage of me," Jouralmon confessed. "I can't seem to recall our meeting. That's a weakness of mine, however—I forget names and faces."

"Peshawar," Gibney murmured. "Get it yet? No. Oh well, you'll recall it after a while. I know you will."

"Perhaps." Jouralmon yawned. "I've been so many places, seen so many people, you know—" But Hearle saw that, try to hide it though he would, Jouralmon remembered now.

Gibney chatted for a few minutes, mostly concerning the possibilities of the trout fishing, in which the Senator seemed to be much interested. Then he nodded to the others, turned away, moved toward the barn again. Jouralmon stood staring after him, a faintly puzzled light in his eyes. Gibney walked with a swinging stride that was rather unusual—one leg was slightly lame, Hearle decided. An odd walk, that, once seen, could not be easily forgotten.

Sudden full recognition, memory, leaped to Jouralmon's eyes. It was as though, half-understanding
before, something had been made quite clear now.
He shrugged, as if to himself, turned away. But
Hearle had seen the startled light that accompanied
memory.

In the house, a telephone was ringing insistently,
a jangling sound that seemed out of place here in
the solitude of the mountains. It stopped, a maid
came to the door.

"Mr. Hearle is wanted on the telephone," she
explained. "A call from the county attorney at
Helena."

Hearle hurried in. Critton, plainly very much
excited, was on the other end of the wire.

"That you, Hearle?" he demanded. "Are you
out at the ranch? Everyone else there—Jouralmon
too? Oh, I know that Yamamoto didn't go out with
you. That's what I called you up about. There's
something mighty queer about this whole thing,
if you ask me. Lee Hung has just reported that
Yamamoto and his cousin, Pin H'sueh, are out
at his house—dead. They seem to have murdered
each other."

CHAPTER XX

Jouralmon expressed himself as horrified at the news, but to Hearle, this did not seem to ring quite true. It was as though Louis Jouralmon had expected the news, had set himself to play the part, and played it, like a polished actor. It was good acting. But that was all.

Here, unless Hearle was badly mistaken, was the hand that pulled the strings, and when he jerked them his puppets danced. They did the dirty work, but a craftier brain conceived and planned every move in advance. Of course, he might be entirely wrong, be doing Jouralmon an injustice in his thoughts, Hearle realized. He had a theory which seemed to hang together. But of tangible proof, of motive for all this hideous chain of crime, he had nothing at all.

It would have been easy enough, even logical, if his suppositions were correct, for Yamamoto to have murdered Kasmin. But why should he do it? Why? Why should he, a Japanese servant, desire to do away with Kasmin? Or, if he murdered at the bequest of his master, what possible motive could Jouralmon have for desiring the death of the gangster? Others appeared to have good reasons for desiring to see him disposed of, or at least to have been on none too cordial relations with him.

171

But this did not apply in the case of Jouralmon. Why should he have wanted Kasmin killed?

Yet Kasmin had been murdered, and there was a weak link in the chain. Next, Sargent had been murdered. Here again, it seemed that Yamamoto might be implicated, and if so, that he must work with the knowledge of and at the behest of his employer. But again, there seemed to be no tangible reason back of it all, no logical motive.

Assuming, however, that this was so—that Yamamoto had done these things at the orders of Jouralmon, and for the moment forgetting the motive, much became clear. Yamamoto had been assisted in his second crime by Pin H'sueh, which meant that Pin H'sueh's tale of what had occurred in the Roses of Fragrant Gardens restaurant, in San Francisco, and his subsequent reason for being in Helena, was in all probability a falsehood—though again, Kasmin and Sargent had been together in that back room in San Francisco, and there might be a hidden reason for it all, in fact. But it appeared that Pin H'sueh was also in the employ of Jouralmon, and had come to Helena, not for the purpose of visiting his cousin, but to be of definite use in the commission of a crime.

After that, his weakness had led to his downfall. His fondness for the opium pipe had betrayed him to Hearle, had made Yamamoto nervous and angry the night before. This morning, Yamamoto had gathered that Hearle knew too many things which were supposed to be hidden—dangerous things. His assumption, which Hearle had encouraged him in, was that Pin H'sueh had told those things, while under the influence of the drug—that it had

172

acted upon him as liquor does upon some men, making him drunk and loosening his tongue.

Yamamoto had no way of knowing how much Pin H'sueh might have told when in such a condition. But if he had talked once, he might talk again. Living, he could be a dangerous witness, if fed opium. Dead, he could tell no more. Jouralmon had listened to Yamamoto's report, of what he feared and suspected, had told Yamamoto to go on an errand—and, in a few words of dialect, had made sure that Yamamoto understood what that errand really was to be, had ordered Yamamoto to kill Pin H'sueh, thereby stopping his tongue forever.

Yamamoto had been very willing to obey, since he realized all too clearly that his own safety and life were imperiled by Pin H'sueh remaining alive. But Jouralmon had considered that they had both served his ends, were both dangerous alive, to his own well being. If one man dead could tell no tales, certainly two could tell even less!

So, having sent Yamamoto to murder Pin H'sueh, he had proceeded to telephone to Pin H'sueh, talking to him in Pin H'sueh's own language, according to the remark of the telephone girl—a circumstance worth bearing in mind—and had warned Pin H'sueh that a rabid Yamamoto was coming. Jouralmon had advised him, unquestionably, to kill Yamamoto.

And the two of them had obeyed orders, exactly as Jouralmon had counted upon! Naturally, he was not surprised by the news he heard.

It all had a very logical sound, but for that reason, Hearle was inclined to be distrustful of it.

173

Everything fitted together too smoothly. And after all, everything that he had seen and interpreted in this manner might have an entirely different meaning. He still had only theories to go on, not facts. And theories, he had long ago learned, are treacherous material out of which to build a case that will stand against the storms inevitably to arise in court. Either he was right—or he was altogether wrong.

Staying at the ranch only for lunch, Hearle and Jouralmon, with a chauffeur to drive them, returned to town. It was a silent ride. Hearle was preoccupied with his own thoughts, and Jouralmon likewise seemed to be busy in thinking over past events. Was he riding with an arch-criminal, Hearle wondered, or with an innocent man? Though he might not commit the crime with his own hands, a man who could engineer the things that had happened during the past week, was a far greater criminal than the puppets to whom he was master.

As ever, Jouralmon was politely courteous and considerate even of small points. He did not have either the look or manner of a criminal. Placed in a rural community, he could have posed as squire and leading deacon in the church. But outward appearance meant very little, Hearle knew.

In the city again, they were met by Critton, who told them what there was to know. During the forenoon, Yamamoto had come to the house of Lee Hung, and had inquired there for Pin H'sueh. At the moment, the other members of Lee Hung's household had been elsewhere about their own business, and Lee Hung himself had been about to

174

leave for an hour or so. Since Yamamoto, though a stranger to Lee Hung, had assured him that he was acquainted with Pin H' sueh, who was at the moment sprawled comfortably at ease in an inner room, Lee Hung had bade him enter, had called to Pin H'sueh that he had a visitor, and departed.

Of his household, Lee Hung was the first to return, something more than an hour later. The house was as quietly peaceful as when he had left it, and at first he had believed it to be quite deserted, even by Pin H'sueh. But in the room where Pin H' sueh had been reclining, at ease when Yamamoto called, Lee Hung found the two of them. A short, evil-bladed dagger, that could almost be hidden in the palm of the hand, was in Yamamoto's grasp still, its point buried in Pin H'sueh's heart. Pin H'sueh's powerful hands were about Yamamoto's neck, which had been broken cleanly.

The two of them; when discovered by Lee Hung, were locked together, face to face, upon their knees. Hatred seemed to be the predominate expression graven upon each countenance, the mask of life having been ripped away in those last terrible moments. Evidently they had been standing, face to face, and Yamamoto had thrust with his dagger, without warning, finding his mark. Even then, in the grip of death, Pin H'sueh had been swift, had caught him and broken his neck with a single twist of his powerful hands. Locked together, they had sunk down to their knees, their embrace preventing them from falling altogether.

It was, quite clearly, a case of double murder. Hearle questioned Lee Hung about the events of the morning. But Lee Hung had been outside of

175

his house a good part of the morning before Yamamoto had called. If there had been any telephone call, then Pin H'sueh must have answered it himself, for Lee Hung knew nothing of it.

Jouralmon, questioned by the coroner, declared that he had sent Yamamoto on an errand to a little store on Broadway that morning, described it in detail. Hearle, as witness, corroborated him in this. Why Yamamoto had come to the house of Lee Hung and asked for Pin H'sueh, Jouralmon could not surmise. Certainly, Yamamoto had disobeyed explicit orders to go to the store on Broadway, and then to hurry back to the waiting cars.

The double murder being so self-evident, though in the case of one of them, probably Pin H'sueh, it looked like self-defense, Dr. Strait announced that there would be no inquest. Hearle agreed with him in this matter. Jouralmon explained that he would use the rest of the afternoon in making arrangements for the disposition of Yamamoto's body and in writing a letter to the only relative of the dead man that he knew of, a sister in the Philippines. Since his own servant had been responsible for the death of Lee Hung's cousin, he would also pay the funeral expenses for Pin H'sueh. He would be ready to go back to the ranch the next morning, and that arrangement was satisfactory to Hearle as well, who called up Leadley at the ranch. The latter announced that the pack-trip back into the deeper hills would accordingly be postponed until Monday.

Jouralmon departed about business of his own, and Hearle, accompanied by Critton, checked up on his story at the store on Broadway. But if Hearle had expected to find this a pure fiction, he was disappointed. The proprietor agreed with the story as told by Jouralmon. Though that, as Hearle knew, might mean anything or nothing. If Jour-almon was really the master-criminal that Hearle considered he might be, he would have found ways to attend to such a detail as this.

"What do you think of it all, anyway?" Critton asked. "You know a lot more about this case than you're telling, Hearle. As for me, I'll confess that I'm getting in deeper all the time. This murder of these Chinks today, by each other, must have some bearing on the case, but it all looks foolish to me."

"It does look so. I do have some opinions, but they have been so frequently upset in the past, that I'm not saying anything unless I know what I'm talking about."

"I don't blame you any. I wish I'd had sense enough to follow that rule in the past. It would have saved me getting my fingers badly burned."

The next morning, Hearle and Jouralmon drove back to the ranch again. Everything was as they had left it, quiet and peaceful with the silence of the far places, where no railroad, no passing motor cars, not even the hum of an airplane, inter-vened. Jouralmon declared, with a sigh, that he hoped it would remain peaceful. It was the most trying, nerve-racking vacation that he had ever been on. At that moment, he looked like a tired, rather old man, infinitely weary. Hearle felt a pang of doubt. His case, after all, appeared to be built upon very trifling supports.

Jouralmon alighted from the car, walked off by himself a few steps. Hearle, moving after him, had a sudden look at his face. Jouralmon was staring straight before him, sheer terror reflected in his eyes, his face a pasty white, his fingers closing and unclosing. He raised a hand to his collar, as though it chocked him.

Hearle looked to see what could be the cause of this. Beyond was a wooded hillside, fragrant with the spicy tang of the pines. Nearer at hand, the trout stream ran softly, deeply. Still closer, Senator Ferguson and Mr. Gibney were walking quietly along, chatting casually, each with a fly-rod in his hand, quite evidently bent on fishing. There was nothing else in sight, nothing that seemed at all out of place with the peaceful Sabbath.

CHAPTER XXI

The trail back to the farther recesses of Leadley's ranch was one to make any dude, seeking the rugged West, feel that he was getting his money's worth. Leadley did not own the country back in here, as he explained to Hearle, much of it being located in the forest reserve. He had, however, made arrangements with the government to lease part of it, the pasturage in some sections for his cattle, the rest, under careful guides, for the use of his dude ranch. Cabins had been constructed far back, almost at the foot of a glacier. In return, Leadley's crew were charged with keeping everything in the best of condition, and guarding against forest fires on that section of the reserve.

Now and again the trail wound along sheer precipitous ledges, where a slip of one of the horses would have meant death far below. Up and down it wound, over towering mountains and descending again into deep gorges. In the bottoms of these the sunlight came for only a few scant hours on the longest mid-summer days. In winter, many of them never beheld the sunlight at all, and dusk hid the recesses at midday. Here were icy, plunging trout streams, deep pools of magic; an air heavy with the odor of pine. On the higher peaks, drifts of snow would linger until mid-summer, and miniature glaciers were plentiful now. The necessary ten miles or so required four hours to cover.

A deer paused in the trail ahead to survey them,
unafraid. Farther on, a bear ambled along the
mountainside and into the shade of the forest.

Three cowboy-guides accompanied them, and two
maids and a cook had been sent ahead a few days
before. Gibney likewise went along to supervise
things, proving that he was adept at whatever
turned up. More than once, Hearle caught himself
marveling at the strength of the little man. He
seemed literally to be made of steel. Yet there
was something puzzling, unapproachable, about
him. A strangeness behind which the real man
himself dwelt, aloof, sheltered from a curious world.
He might have been, still might be, anything.

Hearle enjoyed the trip in. He had ridden enough
at various times that he was no novice. The
others too, he noted, with the single exception of
Pinard, seemed to get along very well with a horse.
Pinard did not, though he endured cheerfully and
made no comments. Mrs. Reid grumbled a good
deal, but without really appearing to mean it. She
seemed, in fact, to be an excellent horsewoman, as
were all three girls and Dolores Dixon. Jouralmon
was, he explained, comparatively pleased whenever
he had a horse to travel with. He had tried camels,
elephants and other methods sufficiently to consider
a good horse as an almost priceless gift. The
Senator heartily seconded him in this.

Here, far removed from sight and sound of
civilization, the nightmare of the past week began to
recede like a dim, fanciful shadow. Only the
white, carefully schooled face of Joan Sargent was a
reminder, though she was no kill-joy for the others.

Most of them lounged about camp during Mon-

day afternoon, resting aching muscles. **On Tues-**
day, however, everyone was ready to go fishing.
There were two streams near at hand, both of
which Leadley declared, would furnish sport to
satisfy even a president, and a little lake was set
a couple of miles away in the hills. Soon the
whole party had scattered widely.

Eric Hearle had put the matter of the crimes
definitely out of his mind for the day, determined
to relax and rest, so as to attack it with new vigor
presently. He preferred to wander off by himself,
fishing with no one, not even a guide, near at hand.
The trout, as Leadley had declared, were joyously
ready to bite, rising in a way to thrill the most
phlegmatic fisherman, and Hearle was far from
apathetic. There were not many big ones, the
average catch running around ten inches. But
they were game, and often gave him a battle royal.
By mid-afternoon he had a well-filled creel, and
picked his way back toward the cabins.

As he had already discovered, the going was
not of the best. There were almost no man-made
trails in here, and the mountains and trees, to say
nothing of occasional underbrush, had a way of
interfering. Accordingly, dusk was falling when
he finally reached camp. Nearly everyone else was
in by then, Leadley and Jouralmon alone being
out. A steaming supper was waiting, and as the
other guests, not standing on ceremony, had already eaten, Hearle fell to ravenously. He was
half through the meal when Leadley arrived.

Darkness began to fall, and still Jouralmon was
missing. He had been fishing near the lake, as had
several of the others, though each one had struck

out for himself. The others had finally made their way back to camp, expecting him to do the same.

"We'll take horses and ride over there," Leadley decided. "Get the men, Gibney, and I'll go with you."

"I'll go, too," Hearle said, but Pinard shook his head.

"I'd like to," he confessed. "But I can't keep up on foot, and I wouldn't ride a horse again today unless it was a case of life and death." He smiled wryly. "I'm so sore from yesterday that I hate myself," he added.

Senator Ferguson also decided to remain at camp. The others, following Leadley's lead, made good time back to the lake. By now, an early moon had come up, and it gave sufficient light to see fairly well, making a shining, dark-luster mirror of the lake, cradled in the hills, with dark pine forests dipping down to the water's edge, single trees standing now and again like great, ghostly sentinels.

"We may as well divide," suggested Gibney. "Half of us ride one way, circling the lake, the other half the other way, so that we'll meet at the far end; and spread out a little."

His suggestions were followed, three men riding each way. Gibney, Hearle and one of the guides circled to the right, the others to the left.

"Don't see what can be wrong with him," the guide complained. "There's no reason for anything to happen to him, or for him to get lost either, in here. I thought he was an experienced traveler in wild places, anyway."

Hearle said nothing. He was recalling the sudden, unexplained terror that had been in Jouralmon's face for a moment, on their arrival at the ranch Sunday. It didn't fit, someway, for Jouralmon to be terrified—not if he was the man that Hearle had thought that he might be. If he was terrified, then somewhere, in his reasoning, Hearle had slipped a cog, which threw everything out of mesh again. And it was almost a week to the hour now since John Kasmin had met his death with a dagger in his heart, back in the Last Chance Hotel. Almost a week to the minute!

Hearle shook himself angrily. It wouldn't do to get superstitious, whatever else he did. This seemed, tonight, a fit setting for the uncanny. But very logical, coldly calculating men were back of all that had happened, or that would happen.

They pushed forward for nearly a mile farther, searching, calling occasionally. Finally, in a little open glade among the big trees, the three of them came together again, while a shout indicated that Leadley and the other two men had almost joined them. And there they found him.

It was a place of big trees, monster pines which had been sheltered by the natural location from the fiercer wrath of the elements, trees which had stood for hundreds of years. A big, partly rotted log lay at the foot of one, and on that, his side against another tree, which had kept him from falling to the ground, sat Louis Jouralmon. A long, evil-bladed Chinese dagger, very similar to that which had taken the life from John Kasmin, was in his back, penetrating to the heart.

He was staring straight ahead and upward a little, at another big tree perhaps six feet in front of him,

183

staring as with a curious fascination. Sticking in it, in direct line with his eyes, was another dagger, its point buried three inches deep in the bark and wood of the soft pine tree. On Jouralmon's face, as he stared at this, was a look of almost incredible horror. It had been graven there in swift death.

The three had stopped as by mutual consent, and sat in their saddles, staring. The moon gave a luminous, soft light that was easy to see by. Now Hearle gave a swift word of command to keep back, and dismounted carefully from his own horse. Neither of the two men with him had said a word at the discovery. On their faces, he noted, was a look of shocked horror, of blank incredulity. From beyond, Leadley's horse plunged through a line of trees into sight, was jerked to an abrupt standstill.

"My God," Leadley cried. "Jouralmon too!"

"The Golden Bowl has been broken again," Hearle nodded. "Death has claimed him—sometime before darkness settled, I should say."

Leadley called a word of warning to his companions, to keep back, so as not to disturb any sign which might exist. Hearle stood still for a moment, looking carefully about, then drew a flashlight from his pocket and studied everything in greater detail. A little spring bubbled out from under a mossy rock not far off, started bravely out to join with the lake, some hundred paces distant, but was quickly lost as it spread, almost into a little bog. The ground, accordingly, was quite soft hereabouts, and would show footprints clearly.

Those of Jouralmon were readily visible in the soft ground, showing how he had walked toward the log, intent on resting. His fishing rod and creel he had laid down, apparently, beside the foot of the log, when he sat down. No other marks were anywhere near the log at all.

Perhaps a dozen feet behind where Jouralmon sat, the influence of the little spring was lost, and here again the ground was hard and dry, carpeted with a thick layer of brown pine needles. Someone had approached softly from behind, unheard in these, but the trail that he had made was so indefinite as to be valueless. It might have been made by any man on the ranch—or any woman, or a total stranger.

"Whoever did it, came up behind him, and stuck a knife in his back without giving him a warning, or any chance," Leadley muttered hoarsely, "man, what sort of a devil are we up against?"

"A very ingenious one," Hearle answered. "But it wasn't quite as you picture it. Whoever did it, didn't exactly stick that knife in his back—not with his hands. He threw it, from the edge of this dry ground."

"It would take an expert to do that—and get the heart at the first shot," Leadley grunted. As by a common impulse, his eyes and those of Hearle turned toward Gibney. But he was leaning forward in the saddle, staring, and appeared not to notice.

"Certainly, very few men could do it," Hearle agreed. "But even then, it wasn't quite as you suggested, Leadley. He didn't murder Jouralmon entirely without warning. First, he threw that other dagger, which is sticking into the tree. It wasn't thrown at Jouralmon, a poor shot, but was tossed into the tree deliberately. It meant some-

thing to Jouralmon—just what, we can only guess.
It might have told him as much as a book could
tell us. Again, he may have merely understood
that death stood behind him, as any of us might,
now, in similar circumstances, and knowing what
we do. But he had that warning. Perhaps his
slayer spoke to him as well. Jouralmon knew that
death stood behind him. You can see it written
upon his face.

"After he knew, death came, when the second
dagger was thrown. Death, as in the case of John
Kasmin, was instantaneous. And both men seem
to have known in advance that death was close upon them."

CHAPTER XXII

Back at the cabins again, Hearle was busy for a few minutes in examining the two daggers for finger-prints—an art in which he had had considerable experience. He was neither greatly surprised nor disappointed to discover that these two daggers, like the other articles in this chain of crime, contained no tangible clues.

Louis Jouralmon had been laid out in an inner room, awaiting the arrival of the coroner, which could not possibly be until well into the next day. The news of this latest murder had produced a palling effect upon the other guests; a sense of the fear of the unknown was beginning to lurk in the back of their eyes. Here, in the depths of the wilderness, such a killing somehow seemed worse than in a crowded hotel.

Before retiring for the night, Hearle questioned Leadley concerning Gibney.

"We really haven't any cause to suspect him, except the fact that he has known Jouralmon at some time in the past, and his ability as a knife-thrower," Hearle explained. He did not mention the terror which had lurked in Jouralmon's eyes on Sunday when, as Senator Ferguson and Gibney were going fishing, Jouralmon had evidently seen or

187

remembered something from a dim past, something which terrified him.

"The way those knives were thrown automatically eliminates a lot of possible suspects," Hearle added.

"And appears to implicate Gibney," Leadley amplified. "To tell the truth, I don't know anything about him. But I did discover something only this afternoon which didn't seem to be important then, but looks now as though it might be. One of the guides told me that Gibney had been in to Helena two or three times last week, though Gibney didn't mention that to me when I saw him. Of course, there was no reason why he should. He's general manager here, and has a lot of things to look after, with perfectly logical reasons for making a lot of trips to town.

"Besides that, he was gone more or less at night. No one really knows where he was, most of the time last week. He might have been in Helena when we didn't suspect him."

"Do you suspect him?" demanded Hearle.

Leadley shook his head.

"I don't, no. And yet, in this last case, at least, it looks funny to me. I just thought, in view of what had happened, that you ought to know how things shape up. That's all."

"It's worth considering," Hearle agreed.

The next morning, he took up his investigation again in earnest. It developed that, besides himself, Joan Sargent, Mrs. Reid and Pinard had devoted themselves to creek fishing the day before. The others had all been fishing somewhere about the lake, but even so, it would have been easily possible for anyone to pass along the lake shore while Jouralmon sat dead on his log, and never suspect his presence.   Anyone could have been guilty, by a little clever maneuvering as to time and place, and those appearing to be most innocent, or at the greatest distance from the lake, might as easily have been guilty as those who had been close at hand.

Again, it appeared that Jouralmon had been killed late in the afternoon—at which time, most of the party had either returned to the cabins or were on their way there, generally traveling in twos or threes.   But even this was only guess work, and gave no one a clear alibi.   The possibility that some outsider, not even known of, might be guilty, Hearle dismissed without consideration.   It was, all too plainly, someone who was known.   That was where the danger came in, and Hearle recognized it as a very real peril to be faced and met.

It had seemed to him, a week before, that the crime pointed to Richard Sargent as guilty, although the fact had not seemed probable to him.   But Richard Sargent had been the second man to be murdered, and it had been clearly established since then that he was not guilty.   So, again, the evidence had seemed to point in the direction of Louis Jouralmon's servants, and of Jouralmon himself. Yet now the servants and Jouralmon were dead, even as Sargent had been killed.   The whole series seemed linked up together, with the criminal still unsuspected in their midst, fiendishly clever, with an apparently insatiable blood-lust.   In that case, the end might not yet have been reached.

Gibney, at Hearle's request, came in for questioning. He smiled a little as he came, though there was a trace of bitterness in the smile.

"You're suspicious that I threw those daggers," he stated without preamble. "Leadley has told you, of course, of my ability as a knife-thrower. I picked it up as a hobby, years ago, in the far East—and I've kept it up, since it has saved my life a time or so, and such useful hobbies appeal to me. However, I didn't toss those knives yesterday. But I did have opportunity enough, and I have no alibi that would be worth a cent."

"It wasn't that which I wished to talk to you about," Hearle explained. "Of course, you could have been guilty, so far as opportunities are concerned. But so might some of the others. I wanted to ask you what you knew about Jouralmon, in the past. I think that you claimed to have met him a good many years ago, in Peshawar. You might know something about him that would furnish someone with a motive for desiring to murder him?"

"Motive enough, and a motive, which, as a man of honor, might apply to me," Gibney nodded. "Yes, it was at Peshawar, on the Northern frontier of India. That must have been about fifteen years ago, or such a matter. Peshawar is a frontier town, you know, an outpost against the wild Mohammedan hordes of the vast country lying to the North and West. They are nomadic tribes, in general, with few restraints, fierce fighting men who have cast covetous eyes down on India for a long time. They would sweep down in vast numbers almost overnight, if England relaxed its vigilance. Conse-

190

quently, it requires real fighting men, both English and native, to hold the border.

"I had just finished a term with the French Foreign Legion," Gibney went on. "And from that I drifted, more or less naturally, to Peshawar. I've always had a fondness for far places. And having been in the Legion, accustomed to some wild places myself, I got on very well with the British officers stationed there.

"It was rather a dull time at the moment—not much unrest or excitement, and naturally the officers gambled a good bit among themselves. I joined in, having a little money. And at about that time, Jouralmon appeared in town with his two Chinese servants."

"Chinese servants?"

"Yes. One of them was a big fellow from the North of China, powerful as an ox, named Pin H'sueh. I have a good memory for names and faces. The same fellow, I gather, that was murdered by Yamamoto in town the other day—and Yamamoto was the other one. A Chinese with a Japanese name, which helped me to remember them, for that's an odd combination, considering the racial antipathy. Strange world, isn't it? Good servants, and hating each other cordially, I gathered, but working together none the less. One sees some queer combinations, in knocking around the world.

"Jouralmon was seeing the country, it seemed, and had just come up from the south. He was a millionaire, I gathered, and for the first few days of his stay he got on very well with the officers. Presently he was sitting in with us on our games. The man loved to gamble. You could see the fever of it get into his eyes, even though he had a natural poker face. And he was almost always lucky at cards. Too lucky, some thought.

"Anyway, it got to the point where he had made some tremendous winnings—winnings that, if he was a millionaire, he certainly had no need of, which counted on the other side as losses that most of the officers could very ill afford. I dropped five thousand pounds to him myself on the last big night of play—such a night as you hear about, but encounter only once in a wild lifetime. The stakes ran high, that night, boosted up by Jouralmon. When we quit, the stars were sinking out for the dawn, and he was a hundred thousand pounds— half a million dollars, the winner. And everybody else was cleaned out. Some of the fellows were irreparably ruined. Two of them, I know, took the easiest way out—suicide. One was sent home in disgrace at the start of a remarkably promising career.

"Our heads were a bit fuddled that morning, I guess, after a long night of the cards and a bit too much wine. But towards night, after we had had some sleep, some of us began to compare notes. It wasn't long until suspicion became almost a certainty. Such luck wasn't possible, on the face of it. And then there were other things. One or two turned up later that afforded the proof. Jouralmon's luck was something more than luck—he had cheated. Ruined three men at the least, and was really responsible for the death of two. But when we came to look for him, he had been gone for hours. I never saw or heard of him again until here the other day."

"So that's his record, eh? I dont know that I would have blamed you very much if you had thrown those daggers."

Gibney shrugged.

"It would have served him right," he admitted. "But all that I lost, personally, was my money. I was broke, but that was rather an habitual experience with me. All that I had to do was start over again, so I didn't entertain any great personal bitterness. Of course, I had been robbed. But a man who gambles can expect that to happen more often than not. Why blame the other fellow because you're a fool?"

"Did you know him then under the same name?"

"Jouralmon? Yes. After he had disappeared, of course, nothing was ever said, and Peshawar is a far outpost. No special need for him to change his name or try to hide. Chances are that I'm the first man there to meet up with him again."

"You didn't see anything suspicious, yesterday?"

"Can't say that I did, no."

After Gibney had left the room, Hearle sat staring silent into space for a few minutes, considering. The body of Jouralmon lay in the next room, that terrible expression of horror and terror still graven on his face. More than one of the guests had studied him with a curious sort of fascination. That look on his face seemed somehow to change his whole appearance—to make him, in death, appear rather terrible—as though the cloak that he had worn through life had been swept away.

A small sound in the next room caused Hearle to get to his feet and move to the doorway connecting the two rooms. Someone was standing there, staring down at Jouralmon. A shade had been drawn, and the shadows lay heavily in that second room, so that at first Hearle could not see well. Then he made out that it was a woman who stood looking down at Jouralmon, her back turned to Hearle, quite unconscious of his presence. His eyes becoming accustomed to the gloom, Hearle recognized Dolores Dixon.

Presently she turned away, moved slowly toward the farther door by which she had entered. There she paused for a moment, turned back for one last look. Hearle had a clear view of her face. He was startled by what he saw there. Feeling herself unobserved, she was not the polished actress now hiding her feelings under a mask which meant something else.

In her eyes and face, as she looked at the dead man, was such a searing, implacable hatred and loathing as Hearle had never before seen on any human countenance.

CHAPTER XXIII

Sheriff Oliver, Coroner Strait and Mr. Critton arrived shortly after midday, having been several hours on the road and trail. With their arrival, a new tension seemed to settle down upon the party. Here, even more than that silent figure in a back room, was tangible evidence that the whole case was far from ended—that it was, in fact, making a grim and steady progress from one death to another. The realization of this was like the appearance of an intangible terror; hysteria came very close to gripping many members of the party.

"I hadn't stopped to consider it before," Mr. Pinard confided to Hearle. "But we seem to be up against an insatiable killer. Where will the whole thing stop? It has driven my wife almost to a nervous breakdown. I never saw her so badly upset as she is now."

Dr. Strait, having examined her, declared that she must be gotten back down to the main ranch house, and given absolute rest and quiet for a few days. Any added shock or disturbance would result disastrously.

"We came up here for a rest and vacation,"

195

Pinard muttered gloomily. "She has been working on sheer nerve for several weeks, to finish up the last picture we made, and now this is too much. I certainly hope that nothing else happens."

Hearle made no comment. Was this sudden breakdown and hysteria a clever pose, he wondered, or was it the real thing? Dolores Dixon was a clever actress. She might fool even a reputable physician. In any case, it prevented him from questioning her for a while, and he had been very sure that she could throw light on the subject, if she would.

Denied that opportunity, Hearle turned to Mrs. Reid. During the last few days much of her gay frivolity had departed; a strained, almost terrified look dwelt in her eyes.

"I somehow can't get over the feeling that I'm responsible for all of this," she almost whispered. "I wished for a murder—though I swear I never meant it—and look what has followed. It—it haunts me."

"You are overwrought," Hearle replied calmly. "As a matter of fact, you have nothing to blame yourself for. I know that you are not responsible for anything that has happened."

Her face brightened a little. A shallow woman, Hearle reflected, easily swayed in her emotions.

"Oh, you take a dreadful load off my mind by saying that. I—I'm afraid I'm superstitious."

"Show me the man or woman who isn't, placed in the proper environment and circumstances, and I will show you a paragon heretofore unequaled in the history of the world," Hearle smiled. "No, you have no cause to blame yourself for anything.

196

But you can see what I am up against in this case,"
he went on earnestly. "A cold-blooded killer, absolutely without compunction. I need all the information that I can get. And I believe that you
are holding something back that I should know."

"I can't think what, Mr. Hearle."

"In the first place, you had met Mr. Kasmin before that meeting a few weeks ago on the coast?"

"Well—I did meet him down in Florida, last
winter. He was staying at the same hotel, and we
became acquainted. Only very slightly acquainted,
however. I assure you that nothing there could
have any bearing on what has happened up here."

"I'll take your word for it. But why did you
try to make me believe that you had never known
him before?"

"Why, I was afraid of the publicity. His being killed, and everything seemed so horrible—
and that seemed so unimportant."

"I understand. Now, Mrs. Reid, please tell me
the truth. What did you know of Louis Jouralmon, in the past?"

"Nothing. I never even heard of him until we
met on this trip."

"And Mr. Sargent?"

"Only what I have told you before."

"What relation are you to Senator Ferguson?"

"No relation, save that of an old friend of his
wife's. Accordingly, I was friendly with his
daughters, and he asked me to come west with
them, when he found that he was delayed longer
than he had expected to be, in Washington."

"Pardon my bluntness, please, Mrs. Reid; but

you are in rather straitened circumstances, financially?"

Mrs. Reid colored slightly, but her eyes were steady.

"That is true. My first husband left me a considerable fortune. Like a fool, I married a gambler —who left me—nothing. I have had to make my own living, since then, in the only way I know— as a paid chaperon, and so on."

"Mr. Reid was your first husband?"

"Yes. I—after my second had left me, I secured a divorce, and took my first married name again."

"What was the name of your second husband, if I may ask?"

"Edwards."

"Edwards? He had, of course, no connection with anyone in this party, in any way?"

"No connection, no."

"You are very patient with me, Mrs. Reid. How long have you known Senator Ferguson?"

"About ten years."

"And his wife has been dead about how long?"

"About five years."

"Was he ever acquainted, do you know, with any of the other members of this party, with the exception of Mr. Leadley?"

"Not that I know of."

"Thank you, Mrs. Reid. I'm sorry to have troubled you."

Hearle was disappointed. He had been confident, from the first, that Mrs. Reid could throw more light on the subject than she had done. The knowledge that she had not at first told the full truth of her acquaintance with Kasmin had strengthened his belief that she was holding something back. But that was satisfactorily explained. A rather shallow woman, she was pleased with attentions from any man with money, even such a man as Kasmin. She appeared to be telling the truth. After all, she was only what she appeared to be.

By this time, the three officers had had a bite to eat, had surveyed the body of Jouralmon, and asked various questions. Critton sought out Hearle.

"Well, we're up against it again, eh?"

"So it would seem."

"Murder, sheer murder—and it gets worse all the time," Critton groaned. "What's to be done next?"

"I've been rather waiting for you to help me out with a possible experiment or so," Hearle said. "Are you ready for some work now?"

"I'm ready to stick on this case from now till doomsday, if necessary," Critton replied savagely. "And if we do find out anything, it looks as though doomsday might sound for us soon, too."

"It might, at that," agreed Hearle. "We'll look over the scene of the latest crime by daylight."

An hour later they arrived at the spot beside the lake. Leadley had been careful to keep everyone about the place busy where he could be watched that day, so that no one had been given an opportunity, even had he so wished, to bother the evidence in any way. Everything was as it had been the night before.

Hearle explained to Critton how things had been

found, and took from a saddle-bag the fishing rod
and creel that had been found beside Jouralmon.

"I haven't looked these over any yet," he explained. "I wanted you to be here when I did."
He arranged them in approximately the same position in which they had been found, himself sat
down on the log where Jouralmon had been, assumed the same pose as that in which the dead
man had been found.

"These could have been dropped from his hand
after he was killed, or have been placed beside him,
ready to his hand, when he first sat down," Hearle
pointed out. "I'm inclined to think that the creel
was laid down beforehand, but that he must have
continued to hold the rod, so that it fell from his
hand when the dagger pierced his heart."

"It looks that way," agreed Critton, studying the
position of both articles. "That was as dirty a killing as anything I've ever heard of. A tired man
sits down to rest, and is killed by a knife in the
back. I'd like to get hold of the man who did it.
It would be the noose for him."

"We'll keep these things as possible evidence,"
Hearle added, putting the creel and fishing rod back
in his saddle bags. Remember their positions,
please. Just at present, let's study out in detail a
little more, how the crime was committed."

He glanced all around. On all sides save one the
trees closed in, making it impossible to see far. But
down a little leafy avenue in the general direction
that Jouralmon had been facing, it was possible to
see with unobstructed vision for perhaps a hundred
yards, almost to the shore of the lake itself. In
fact, a glint of its sun-dappled waters could be

200

caught now through the thick leaves that served to hide it.

"Let's circle around and investigate a bit," Hearle suggested.

Their circle showed them the tracks made by the horses' hoofs of the searching party the evening before, and a little trail, running along at the very edge of the lake, where one or two fishermen had passed back and forth. Then, at about the end of the leafy avenue, down which Jouralmon might have looked from where he sat, had he been so minded, they discovered a natural path leading up toward that avenue. The horses had not been near this spot, but there were signs that someone had come up that pathway recently—no longer ago than the previous afternoon, certainly.

Moreover, this was not the natural route to be taken by a fisherman, going around the edge of the lake. Although a fisherman might have strayed off into this side-path in the belief that it would lead him back to the water a little farther on.

Only one man had walked here, however; that was plain to see, for the ground here, always slightly moist, contained few leaves, and the tracks made by the man could be clearly seen. One shoe appeared to be more worn than the other.

"Looks like a tramp had made those marks," Critton commented.

"He came just to the edge of this leafy avenue down which Jouralmon could see, and stopped," Hearle pointed out. "He must have discovered Jouralmon, sitting up ahead, then have stepped back to deeper shelter behind some of these thicker leaves, so as to be hidden himself from Jouralmon's view.

201

Three steps backward, you see. Then he evidently was of the mind that Jouralmon had discovered his approach, and he wanted Jouralmon to believe that he was still here, waiting. For he took off his hat and thrust it into that little clump of rose briars, so that Jouralmon, if he looked, could barely see it, and it would look as though the man was still wearing it, waiting here.

"After that, leaving the hat as a decoy for Jouralmon to watch, he circled quietly about, came up behind Jouralmon,—and killed him."

CHAPTER XXIV

Critton looked bewildered.

"How do you know that?" he demanded.

"Easy enough. You can see where he circled back, after leaving his hat. Why should he leave it, if not to hold Jouralmon's attention while he came up on him from behind? And afterward, after he had accomplished his purpose and killed Jouralmon, he returned, stepping very carefully in the same tracks, and got his hat again. But he left an important clue behind when he took it."

"What is it?"

"He was wearing a large, white Stetson hat. That narrows down our field of possible suspects. You will notice the space among the rose-briars, where the hat was fitted, is a rather large, round space. It was as though nature had made this place especially to hold the hat in the proper place and position. Yet the brim of the hat was large enough to fill the space, even to crowd it—which an ordinary-sized hat would not have done. Tiny bits of the felt brim caught on the briars, and are still there. Take a look at it."

Critton studied this evidence a moment, shook his head admiringly.

"That's plain enough, now that you point it out to me," he admitted. "Now if we only knew who wears white Stetsons."

"There were only two men in the entire party

wearing white Stetsons yesterday, or during the trip up here from the lower ranch. So I am inclined to think that they are the only ones who have that sort of hat."

"And they are?"

"Senator Ferguson wore one. Mr. Gibney wore the other."

Critton whistled.

"That rather narrows it down, doesn't it? In fact, I should venture a guess that it solves it entirely. The Senator is, naturally, above suspicion. And Leadley was telling me about Gibney's rather marvelous accuracy in throwing knives. There's not much question but what Gibney is our man."

"It looks rather suspicious for him," Hearle nodded. "Still, it would be just as well to keep quiet about what we have discovered, and see what else we can dig up."

"You're certainly right there," Critton agreed. "I've learned that much during this case, anyway."

"And here's something else that is rather puzzling," Hearle pointed out. "Just what do you make of it? I don't see just now, where it fits in at all."

He indicated a tree, just behind where the man who had followed this path had first stopped, sidestepped. Embedded deeply in the wood was something which Hearle now proceeded, with his penknife, to dig out. It proved to be a long, extremely thin article, made of steel, and resembled a dart. It also bore resemblances to a bullet, but was unlike either.

"Ever see anything like that before?" Hearle demanded.

"Never," declared Critton, examining it curiously. "It's a new one on me."

"Same here," Hearle confessed. "And I've run into a lot of queer things in my day. We'll just keep it, though."

"How about taking up a couple of these footprints in the mud and keeping them as evidence?" suggested Critton.

"A good idea. They might impress a jury. There are some large, flat stones down at the lake shore, that should serve very nicely."

It was near mid-afternoon when they returned to the cabins. Gibney was appearing in the role of chief entertainer to the party just now, sprawling at ease, his white Stetson in his hand. Hearle noted that the brim appeared to be rather scratched— though that might have come from riding through the brush.

Most of the party were grouped in the shade of several patriarchal old trees, listening to his rather droll and colorful stories of his adventures in far places of the world. Hearle noted approvingly that the tension had lightened, at least for the moment. Gibney was a born story teller. Mrs. Reid indulged in a gale of laughter, in which the other auditors joined.

"You've been a regular Robinson Crusoe, Mr. Gibney," Mrs. Reid declared. "You've been everywhere, and have had adventures that would make a lot of this seem tame."

Gibney laughed, shrugged.

"I'd hate to lay claim to being more adventurous than old Crusoe," he denied. "In fact, Robinson Crusoe used to be my favorite character when I was a kid. I used to read about him, talk about him, dream about him. In fact, the kids nicknamed me Crusoe. That book of DeFoe's probably had a lot to do with shaping my destiny."

Senator Ferguson was also wearing his white Stetson. Either both men had easy consciences, or, what was more probable, whoever was guilty did not consider that his hat could be considered as evidence against him. Even the most careful criminals, Hearle had learned, are apt to slip up on some of the simplest things. But the evidence left behind on the rose bush had been hardly visible to the casual eye.

The doctor and sheriff planned to ride back down to the main ranch yet that afternoon, then drive back to the city that night. Hearle and Critton decided to go with them. The others of the party, their nervousness returning as night began to creep down, had likewise decided to return to the main ranch the next morning, and from there go back to Helena.

Night had descended when the four finally came to the city. Hearle wearily sought his bed, but a new day found him ready to answer an excited request from Critton.

"I got to thinking of a point that we've been neglecting for a while," the prosecutor explained. "So I did some phoning last night, and I have a hunch that we're going to get some results this morning. Can you come with me?"

Hearle agreed, and Critton presently arrived with a car to pick him up. As usual, when on a fresh trail, he was filled with enthusiasm.

"Remember that mysterious airplane that left the

city on the night that Sargent was killed?" he asked.
"I was afraid at the time that he had gone to
Canada in it, but when I discovered that Gibney
had been in town more or less last week, in what
seemed to be rather a mysterious fashion, it just
occurred to me to find out about that. I tried to
call up McClusky, who owns the plane, last night,
but I couldn't get him then. I did get his wife,
though, and she said that he had taken a passenger
out to Leadley's dude ranch on that night, a week
ago Tuesday. He will be home this morning himself.

McClusky was home. He was a pleasant-ap-
pearing man of about thirty, a skilled aviator who
had received a baptism of fire in the air over No
Man's Land back in 1918. He listened to Critton
in silence, rasped a hand across the black stubble on
his chin, and frowned.

"I generally feel that what I do isn't anybody
else's business," he stated finally. "But when the
law asks me a question, I suppose that comes first.
Yes, I took Gibney out to his ranch that night.
Rather a ticklish business, landing at night, but
there was a couple of lanterns set out to guide me,
and I knew the field. I got used to almost any
sort of flying years ago, of course."

"What time did you take Gibney out, that
night?" Hearle asked.

"About ten o'clock, I guess it was, when we
left town."

"How did he happen to call on you?"

"I've flown him about at other times. In fact,
I brought him in that evening, about the time it
started to get dark."

207

"You got here at about that time, you mean?"

"Yes."

"How did you happen to go out and get him? Did he call you up?"

"No. I had an appointment from the night before."

"I see. You brought him in to town and took him out the night before—Tuesday—as well?"

"Yes."

Hearle turned to Critton.

"You said Tuesday, though you were speaking of the night on which Sargent was killed, which was Wednesday," he pointed out. "This seems to explain that." He turned back to McClusky.

"Both trips were at about the same hours, each night?"

"Just about."

"Were there any other times that you took him on trips last week?"

"Those were the only ones."

"And what was Mr. Gibney's business in the city at that hour, on those two nights?"

McClusky shook his head. It was quite evident that he hated to answer questions of this sort at all.

"I don't know. That wasn't any of my business."

"So you didn't inquire. And he didn't tell you."

"Not a word."

"Was he wet, or muddy, either night?"

"Pretty wet, yes, on Wednesday night. Kind of muddy, too."

"Did he carry anything with him on either trip?"

208

"He had a small leather bag, something like what doctors carry."

"Both times?"

"Yes."

"How long have you known Mr. Gibney?"

"About two months. I was takin' passengers up one day, and he went up for a ride, then said he'd like to hire me occasionally for a trip."

"What do you charge for a trip out to the ranch, and back?"

"Twenty-five dollars, in the day time. Forty at night."

"Then those two trips cost him eighty dollars?"

"Yes."

"At least half a month's wages for him, I would think."

"About that, I guess."

"Does he hire you that way very often?"

"He had had me get him once during the day time, and take him back again. That was all."

"I see. Just how well do you know him, personally?"

"Well—I try not to get personal. This is a business proposition, carryin' passengers. But then, Gibney has knocked around the world a lot, and I've done some myself. So I've got to know him fairly well."

"You like him?"

"I sure do."

"Call him a friend?"

"Reckon I would."

"Trust him?"

"I would, yes, if he was my friend."

"But if he was your enemy?"

"I wouldn't sleep easy nights, if he had it in for me."

"Then you have no idea what his business was in town, on those two nights?"

"No. And now, damn it, I've told you all I do know. I don't like to discuss a man behind his back—even with the law."

"I appreciate your sentiments," nodded Hearle. "Thank you for your trouble."

"Go to the devil," growled McClusky.

CHAPTER XXV

"That was one worth-while idea of mine, anyway," commented Critton. "The whole thing seems to be tying up now."

"A good idea," agreed Hearle. "And now we'll go to the hotel, I think. I obtained permission from Miss Sargent to examine some of her father's things, which she left there temporarily. I'm interested in his dagger case, chiefly. It was my intention, as soon as I discovered that Kasmin had been murdered with one of Mr. Sargent's daggers, to have a look at that case. But his own death following so swiftly, and then the way other things kept turning up, I forgot all about it, until Jouralmon was killed with a dagger as well."

"I hadn't thought of it, either," Critton confessed. "But it should be well worth looking into."

The personal possessions of Richard Sargent had been left in the same room that he had occupied while alive, nothing having been disturbed. Joan had requested that no one, even the hotel employees, should bother the room in any way. A light coat of dust covered things now. In a bureau drawer they found the dagger-case, and Hearle opened it carefully.

Hearle had also brought along the two daggers that had figured in the death of Louis Jouralmon,

211

and the dagger that had taken the life of Kasmin. Now, with the dagger-case open before them, they examined all of the collection carefully. There were twelve daggers still in the case—intricate, beautiful blades, highly polished, with handles of jade. One compartment in the case was empty—where the blade that had killed Kasmin had reposed.

"He kept thirteen daggers in it, evidently," Critton commented. "Rather a grim thirteen, eh?"

"Sufficiently grim for the casual taste, certainly. I would say, offhand, that these twelve blades had never been used—that is, for the purpose of murder. Now this blade that killed Kasmin, though it has been cleaned quite carefully, shows a slight blood stain yet, near the handle.

"And this blade that was used to kill Jouralmon likewise shows a blood stain—very faint now, but noticeable. And on this one, which was buried in the tree, this dagger at which Jouralmon was staring, you will note also a faint trace of blood stain. An ancient stain, I should say, rather than a recent one."

Critton examined the blades with interest.

"Looks so," he agreed. "And here's something else. The dagger that killed Kasmin, and the dagger at which Jouralmon was looking, seem to be exact duplicates."

"By George, that's so," agreed Hearle. "The whole collection are so very similar that I hadn't noticed that before, but you're right."

"There must be some significance to it."

"Evidently there is. Two such blades, used in such a way, are decidedly unusual."

"Then—" Critton was staring, a new light of

212

excitement burning in his eyes. "The blades being the same, it must mean that the hand that killed Jouralmon is also the same hand that killed Kasmin."

"It could be."

"It must be. We're getting somewhere, Hearle. And if Gibney killed Jouralmon—well, he was in town here on the night that Kasmin was killed— no one knows what for. He was in town on the night that Sargent was killed. And those are the only two nights that he was in town, last week. Of course, Sargent was killed in a different manner, but that doesn't necessarily mean that he was killed by a different man than killed Kasmin and Jouralmon."

Hearle made no comment. He was examining the other daggers carefully, in an endeavor to find a duplicate of the one that had killed Jouralmon.

But none of the daggers matched with this one. One thing, however, Hearle discovered in his search. Hidden under the daggers, was a smooth pocket, its edges nicely covered by the daggers themselves, so that, when they were in place, it failed to show entirely. Slipped inside of this envelope was a plain white envelope, unsealed, and with no address of any kind upon it. Hearle studied it carefully for a moment, opened it. Inside were several sheets of handwriting, with no address or date, and the whole was unsigned. The salutation, however, was unique.

"Dear Crusoe," it ran. Hearle showed it to Critton. The minds of both men reverted to what Gibney had told of himself the day before, out at the ranch. That, as a boy, he had been nicknamed

213

Crusoe. An odd nickname, not at all common. And this salutation was quite evidently a nickname.

"Let's go down to the register and compare this writing with Sargent's signature, when he registered at the hotel," Hearle suggested. A few minutes later they returned to the room. There could be no question that Sargent had written the letter.

Hearle studied it a moment more, noting that the writing and the paper were both fresh. Then he read it aloud.

"It has been a long time since I've written to you, old boy, for reasons which we both understand very well. And still longer since I have been privileged to hear from you. I have often wished that it could be otherwise, far otherwise. When I think of the old days, of our good times together— well, it almost seems as though those twin daggers made each a double killing.

"However, I am not complaining, for, despite all that has had to be endured, I am firmly convinced that it has been worth it. Whether I will mail this letter to you or not, I do not know. I hope to see you soon—I am looking forward confidently to so doing. But it is in my mind to write you this tonight, for something may come between us, preventing us from meeting. That has happened twice before, and there may be a third time. If anything does happen, I will mail this in a few days, so that you may be well informed of what I think is a vital, and, I trust, will prove to be the last chapter in this affair which we have played for so long.

"I am hot on the trail of the enemy of our house, at last. It has been a long, weary trail, with many turnings, many blank walls. You, I know, have encountered these as frequently as have I. But recently I struck a fresh trail, and I have been following it carefully. It has led me here to Helena, Montana. I am with Lon Leadley, the famous movie star, with whom, as I think you know, I have been acquainted for several years. And somewhere here in Helena—whether in or out of the party that is traveling with Leadley, I am not yet sure—is the man we trailed for two decades, across every continent on earth.

"You have a great advantage over me there. You saw him several times in the old days. I never did. If you were here now, I know that you would recognize him when you saw him, whatever disguise he may have adopted, whatever the changes of the years. But, while I know that I have seen him, spoken to him, I do not know who he is. I have my suspicions. And I am sure that a plan of mine will soon discover him to me. When I am certain, then I will act. And you may be sure that I will do a good job, one that will end this up once for all.

"I have a curiously detached mind in respect to what I have to do. Some, perhaps most of the people of the world at large, would call it murder. But I do not consider it in that light at all. My mind goes back to those foul, deliberate murders of long ago—and of the absolute proof that they were murders, nothing is lacking. Again, it goes on to other murders since then, in the course of the years, to consolidate those first deeds of darkness. In the getting of this proof, I have been into strange corners of the earth, have had weird adventures, interviewed strange people. But I se-

cured the absolute proof. Should anything be left
for you to do, you need never doubt that.

"Accordingly, my state of mind in respect to
this is that what I have to do is not murder, but
merely a simple act of justice. The hangman is
not a murderer, but an instrument of the state. I
am convinced that, faced with all the proof, no jury
on earth would decide otherwise than that this is
justice. I know that the Great Judge would so decide. And it is the old law, an eye for an eye and
a tooth for a tooth.

"Besides the memory of those foul murders, I
have before my eyes, these days, other evidence to
steel my intentions—if it were needed. But it is
not. When the moment comes, justice will be
executed, as we pledged each other years ago to do,
whoever came first to the opportunity.

"One thing I have been thankful for. Our
enemy has no cause to suspect me, never having
seen me, never having heard my name, any more
than he has heard yours. The name we cast aside
that justice might one day be achieved was an honorable name, but the names we have taken instead
have become honorable in turn. I have no regrets.

"Unusual things have happened, here in Helena,
already. But unusual things have dogged my foot-
steps ever since I took up this trail, so that I am
becoming quite accustomed to them. A movie was
being taken of Leadley's guests at the dinner table
tonight—myself included. The lights, according
to arrangement, were to be put out for a moment.
They remained out for about two minutes. At
the conclusion, a man from Indiana, whom I have
encountered a few times, and whom I intensely dis-

216

like and mistrust, had my thirteenth dagger sticking in his heart!

"The evidence, of course, points to me. Which
is an annoyance, but does not worry me. But I
am wondering as to how and why. Why was my
thirteenth dagger used? What connection has John
Kasmin with our affairs? I have been wondering
about him for several days. So far as I can see,
he does not fit in. But still he seems to be involved. Or was that dagger intended for my own
heart? I have not yet come to a decision. It
seems more that he had to be disposed of, or that
he was merely a convenient victim, with which to
cause me trouble. Our enemy is ever vigilant.

"While the lights were out, once I discovered that
they were not going on again when they should, I
took a very natural precaution, such as experience
has taught me is wise. Everyone had been asked to
remain seated, but at the risk of appearing a dis-
courteous guest, I did not. And by moving about
a bit, I think that I saved my life.

"So, despite the fact that it seems to me that our
enemy cannot know me, I am doing a good deal
of thinking. Something is amiss. Which is another reason why I am writing this to you. We
may never meet.

"I intend to pursue my investigations swiftly,
however, to act quickly and surely. Tomorrow,
another twenty-four hours, will tell the tale, I
think. After that, if I think it wise, I will mail
this letter to you, or destroy it. I wish that I knew
what to tell you, but I know so much, and yet so
little that is tangible. Anyway, my hand will be
sure.

"Tomorrow evening, I will complete this. There will be more to tell then."

"Tomorrow evening," Hearle muttered. "Yes, there was more to tell—but dead men tell no tales!"

CHAPTER XXVI

That same afternoon, the others of the party returned from the ranch, and again took up quarters at the hotel. These were intended to be more or less temporary. The vacation, as such, had been a sorry failure. But Leadley, though it was, primarily, his vacation and his party, seemed curiously satisfied on the whole. Hearle could guess why. Under the stress of sorrow, tragedy and swift-coursing events, things which might otherwise have taken a long time to come to a head had moved swiftly toward a climax, Joan Sargent, left an orphan by the death of her father, had found a new protector. And Leadley was more than pleased to be accepted in that role.

As soon as permission could be obtained from the authorities, most of the party intended to go elsewhere at once. Leadley voiced a query as to whether this would be possible or not, by the next day. Critton looked inquiringly at Hearle.

"For my own part," he said, "I see no reason why you shouldn't all go when you get ready. Do you, Hearle?"

"I hate to be a damper on the party, but I really think that everyone should plan on enjoying the beauties of this community a little longer," Hearle returned. "We know a little, we guess at a good deal more—and putting it all together, there remains a great deal that we are not yet sure of."

"It looks clear enough to me," Critton protested. "The fact that that letter was addressed to Crusoe— who is, by his own admission, Gibney—seems to tie it all up together. Gibney killed Jouralmon. He may have had what seemed to him an excellent motive, but the law takes small account of motives."

"How then, do you account for Kasmin also being killed with a dagger of the same type?"

"Well, Gibney was in town Tuesday and Wednesday nights both. He could have done it all—"

"Would he have been the one to kill Sargent, too, in that case? If the letter was written to him?"

"I hadn't thought of that. That's another snag, all right. But I've got a new idea. Let's have another look at that dagger-case."

Hearle examined it closely, opened it, worked for some minutes in silence. Finally he gave a little exclamation of triumph. He had found a hidden compartment inside it, and in this was another gleaming dagger. Hearle drew it out, studied it carefully, passed it over to Critton.

"There is no faint, ancient blood-stain upon it, you will notice," he pointed out.

"But what does that signify?"

"A lot, I think. Sargent, and this mysterious Crusoe to whom he wrote the letter, each possessed a dagger—Sargent refers to his as his "thirteenth" dagger,—and those two daggers were used, I am sure, to commit the crimes which Sargent and Crusoe were sworn to avenge. The murderer, being familiar with these daggers long ago, was not adverse to using the one which he found in Sargents dagger-case for further murder.

"But you will note that ancient, blood-stained

220

dagger was not used to kill Jouralmon. Rather, it was stuck into the tree, where he could see it—a message that, it seemed, he could not fail to understand, as the expression on his face signified that he knew what it meant. But it had taken what was considered an innocent life, so it would not be fitting that it should take a guilty life, or was it used for that purpose—at least, that must have been the theory. Another pair of new daggers, exactly alike, were purchased by Sargent and Crusoe, and kept, one by each, for the purpose of vengeance, whichever one should be given the first chance."

"Sounds logical, in a way," admitted Critton. "Though, in the face of what we know, I still don't see the significance."

"There is no great significance, except as a connecting link. This dagger, you will notice, is the twin to the one that killed Jouralmon. I felt sure that there must be a second dagger of the sort, and I wanted to make sure."

Critton stared.

"That would mean that Jouralmon was the man that Sargent was after—though he wasn't sure—"

"It begins to look that way."

"And you've got a soft spot in your heart for Gibney," charged Critton. "You think that, because he has done a killing of this type to avenge an old murder, that it would be a shame to arrest him. But you don't have to bother with that part of it. I'll attend to it, whenever you say the word."

"Well, I do feel rather that way," Hearle admitted. "And you sound rather bloodthirsty yourself. But there are still a few details to clear up yet. If I could just have a talk with Dolores Dixon—"

"I think that you can have that now," declared Leadley. "She is feeling quite a bit better today, since we have returned here. And if that will help to finish things up, so that we can get away, why, I feel sure that she will consent. She is anxious to get away."

"If you will ask her, then—"

Leadley would, and did. Ten minutes later, Hearle was talking to the actress. She seemed very nearly her normal self again, and declared that she was quite up to the task of answering questions.

"I warn you, that I am going to delve into forbidden subjects," Hearle said. "Into your early past. And I must beg you to be frank with me."

A shadow crossed her face, but she nodded.

"Very well," she agreed. "Since it has to be done, I'll tell you anything I can."

"What was your name, then, before you married Mr. Pinard?"

"Why, Dixon," she replied, with faint surprise. "I've been Dolores Dixon all my life."

"Oh. I had assumed that it was merely a stage name. To go back, then. Will you please tell me some of your earliest recollections and experiences?"

"I hate to," she confessed. "They're so unpleasant. I—there was a man and woman, who are rather shadowy figures now. The woman was good to me, the man wasn't exactly unkind to me, but he was to her. They were always quarreling—chiefly over me, I think. I grew to hate him, just because of that. And we were always traveling,

222

it seemed, somewhere or other—always in the most outlandish, far-away places. I hated the whole thing, but I couldn't help myself.

"And then—they disappeared. Just dropped out of my life. I didn't know what became of them. But I was left in the hands of a stern, elderly spinster for a time, who also traveled a good deal, and who, I guess, tried to bring me up properly. But I hated her, too. And then I seem to have been deserted entirely, at an early age. I managed to live—how, I scarcely know. I worked when I could, even begged. Occasionally I was put in some sort of an orphanage, but I hated those even worse, and managed to escape. I'm rather like Topsy—I just grew.

"Finally, I drifted to the coast, got to working around the studios, worked in as an extra a few times. And then Mr. Pinard discovered me, took an interest in me. From then on, everything was different, like living in a new world. The poverty, fear, humiliation, were all gone. I tried to forget those earlier years, that they had ever existed."

"Poor girl," said Hearle, with genuine sympathy. "And then, a few months before you married Mr. Pinard, Mr. Sargent took an interest in you?"

"Yes. He was very friendly, very good to me. He too, seemed to be interested in my past. But I wished to forget it. I made Mr. Sargent go away and quit bothering me. Since then, I have decided that I was very silly and unkind. His interest was a kindly one, and sincere. But I had seen so little of that sort that I distrusted everyone, and I was fiercely determined never to speak of my past to anyone."

"So he really learned nothing?"

"No. I was very unkind to him."

"Under the circumstances, since you had a career and Mr. Pinard to care for you, it probably didn't greatly matter, and I think that Mr. Sargent realized that. He evidently learned enough to be satisfied in his own mind about you."

Dolores Dixon leaned forward suddenly, her eyes very wide.

"Just what do you mean?" she breathed.

"I will explain presently. First, however, another question. Mr. Jouralmon was the man of your early childhood, whom you grew to hate so bitterly?"

Dolores Dixon started. Then she stared in amazement. Finally she nodded.

"Yes," she agreed. "But how did you know that?"

"Mostly luck," Hearle confessed. "I saw your face when you looked at him—after he was dead."

Miss Dixon was instantly on the defensive. Some of the distrust of the whole world, which had been a heritage of her bitter years of struggle, was to the fore now.

"Just what do you want?" she demanded coldly.

Hearle reached forward, took one of her cold hands in both of his.

"To be your friend, Miss Dixon," he assured her sincerely. "You have no need to be afraid of me. As a matter of fact, there was something revealed in his face after he was dead—something so carefully masked while he was living, that, with the lapse of years, you had failed to recognize him while he was alive. But seeing it in his face then, you remembered. And the remembrance called up all the bitter memories of your youth. Am I not right?"

For a long moment she searched his face with questioning eyes, then nodded.

"That is right," she agreed. "I—oh, when I saw him again, I hated him so bitterly! I know it was wrong, and he dead, but I couldn't help it. I was glad—glad, that he was dead."

"I don't blame you," Hearle nodded. "He was one of the greatest monsters ever to walk the earth in human guise. His real name was Tinley. Does that mean anything to you?"

"Tinley?" The girl puckered her brows thoughtfully. "It seems as though I had heard it somewhere—I can't just place it. Why," she cried, "that was the name you used—of the man in that unsolved case of your early days as a detective—the Van Horn case."

"Exactly. I told you that the sister of the Van Horns, and her husband—their name was Long—had been murdered. Also that they left a baby daughter. You are that daughter."

Dolores stared in amazement for a moment. Slowly the bewilderment faded.

"But I—I don't understand."

"It is a very complicated case. But Tinley—or Jouralmon, as we know him, married your father's sister. They took you, after Tinley had hired thugs to murder your parents, and kept you, so as to get hold of the Van Horn millions. Your aunt, who took care of you, was, unquestionably, under the domination of her husband, but she prob-

225

ably did not suspect that he was a villain—not until later.

"Having you in his custody, he got hold of the money. But he was forced to keep out of the way of your uncles, the Van Horn brothers. They had hired me on the case, were working on it themselves all the time. Tinley dared not let you fall into their hands, for fear that they would get themselves appointed as your guardians, and would then have charge of your fortune. Tinley wanted to keep that money under his own control, to use it as he pleased—and he managed to do it. But he had to keep out of their way, which was why there was so much traveling in far, lonely places.

"Your aunt soon began to find out what sort of man he really was, beneath his polished exterior, I suppose. Naturally, there was trouble. Finally, as he had hired your father and mother murdered, so did he hire your aunt, his wife, disposed of. She had probably found out too much about him, and would have placed you, if possible, in the custody of your Van Horn uncles. So he took the safest way out, the one to which his nature naturally turned. Of course, he had never loved his wife, but had married her merely to use as a tool. Her usefulness to him was passed, so he got rid of her.

"After that, he left you in charge of the stern woman that you speak of. She kept you, I suppose, until the money that he had left with her for your care was gone, and then, when he failed to send more, you were turnd adrift upon the world. It meant less than nothing to Tinley, what happened to you. If you died, so much the better, though that was not necessary enough to cause

226

him to have you killed. He had accomplished his purpose, coldly determined upon years before, of securing the bulk of the Van Horn millions for himself.

"You will understand that I am merely guessing at some of these things, but in the main, I know that I am right, for I happen to be familiar with the case, and a letter left by Richard Sargent connects up with it, and tells a great deal, which I had not known before.

"Tinley, of course, dared not continue under his own name. How could he account for you, or his wife, to the Van Horns? Their vengeance was seeking him, they were working steadily to discover whether or not he was guilty of those three murders—and they finally, it seems, found the proof. So, as Jouralmon, Tinley took up life anew. In the intervening years, most of the money seems to have slipped through his fingers."

Dolores Dixon had leaned forward, watching him raptly. Now she sighed.

"I always wondered, who and what I really was," she said.

"You are a Van Horn, by blood," Hearle repeated. "Some of the proudest blood in the country Long was your father's name, also a well-known name. As to Richard Sargent, he was one of your uncles—Richard Van Horn, the younger Van Horn brother. His letter makes that very clear to me, taken with other things that have transpired. He knew who you were, but he was content, once he had found you, because you were in the care of Pinard. So he did not disturb you with the past."

"So he was my uncle," she said softly. "Poor

227

man. Then—then Joan Sargent is my cousin?"

"She is your cousin. I was struck by her resemblance to the Van Horns some time ago—though, never having seen Richard Sargent, or Richard Van Horn, I did not recognize him as a Van Horn, was not sure just who she reminded me of."

Dolores Dixon rose. She smiled up at Eric Hearle, suddenly leaned forward and kissed him. As he drew back, blushing in frank embarrassment, she laughed gaily.

"As the bearer of good tidings, you deserve it," she assured him. "And now, if you will excuse me, I want to go and find my cousin. It's wonderful, after being a nameless waif, to know that you are somebody, and that you have folks."

CHAPTER XXVII

"One thought has occurred to me," said Hearle. He was toying absently with the fishing rod that had been found beside Jouralmon. "It was our decision that Jouralmon had been holding this rod in his hand, while he sat on the log, and that it was dropped from his hand after he was stabbed."

Critton nodded concurrence.

"It looked that way," he agreed.

"Well," went on Hearle, placidly, "just why, if he sat down to rest for a while, and placed his creel beside him, should he continue to hold his rod —so far from water?"

"That does seem queer."

"Very queer, especially when you give a little careful study to the rod. I got to mulling it over. . . . Take a look at the rod."

Critton picked it up, examined it curiously. It appeared, at first glance, to be merely a telescope rod, which had been folded together, so that its total length, closed, was not quite three feet. At a casual glance, it was merely a fishing rod, folded together for convenience in carrying it through the brush. But at second glance it was unusually thick when folded, rather odd in shape, and rather heavy.

"Let's see what it really is," suggested Hearle. He took the tip of the rod, pulled it out, to form a convenient rod some nine feet in length. But even so, it remained very thick and heavy in the handle. Pushing it together again, it became plain that the rod proper occupied only about half of the long, thick handle. The other half of the handle was in reality a cleverly concealed, small-caliber rifle barrel, with an intricately built-in silencer attachment.

"That explains that bullet-like dart which we found in the tree, where the man at the end of the path had stopped," explained Hearle. "The whole thing, of course, has been made to order, and must have cost a neat sum of money. When folded up, it appears very innocent, and yet is really a most dangerous weapon. Ah, here's where you load it, with five more of the darts in a clip. It would be effective up to a hundred and fifty yards, I imagine. You press a little button instead of a trigger. The clip contained six shells originally, but one has been fired.

"A most ingenious weapon. With it, he could kill a man across a room and no one the wiser as to what had really happened. His purpose in resting on the log, you see, was to intercept the mysterious Crusoe, whom he must have known was coming that way—intercepting and murdering him. He did fire one shot, as we have discovered.

"Crusoe was coming up the path, evidently unaware that danger was threatening him. A leafy screen partly served to hide him from Jouralmon. But it is evident that our friend Crusoe was alert, that some sixth sense had warned him of danger ahead, and he stopped, striving to locate it. In that moment, Jouralmon must have taken a chance and

230

fired, but he missed, and the bullet was embedded in the tree, as we found it."

"You think, then," demanded Critton, "that the man who killed Jouralmon, did so after Jouralmon had first attempted to murder him? That he killed, in turn, as you might say, in self-defense?"

"Judge for yourself. Jouralmon's silent bullet must have further served to warn its intended victim. But, being a skilled hunter himself, we have evidence that he did not betray his knowledge that Jouralmon was up ahead, striving to murder him. Jouralmon realized, of course, that he had missed —otherwise he would not have remained seated on the log, waiting a second chance. He was confident that, with the silencer, and himself sheltered from observation behind a big tree so far down the trail, that the other man could not really know that anything was amiss, but would presently come on again. So Jouralmon waited and watched for a second chance.

"The other man carefully furthered this belief on Jouralmon's part. He had taken three careful steps back, and to the side, to a point where he was completely hidden by thick brush. Then he removed his hat and poked it forward, so that it could barely be seen by Jouralmon, the cluster of rose briars holding it in place.

"He knew well that he was in peril of his life, that he had cause to be wary. Leaving his hat for Jouralmon to watch, he moved carefully around, coming upon Jouralmon from behind, and killed him in turn. It was a game of hide and seek, and both men knew it. Jouralmon, however, tried to murder from ambush, without giving any warning,

231

and almost succeeded. His quarry turned the tables on him, but he did not strike without warning. The two daggers prove that. The first one gave warning, explained to Jouralmon what he needed to know—though he may have been told something in words, as well.

"Jouralmon's gun was still in his hand—that innocent little fishing rod, planned for some such fiendish emergency as this. Crusoe evidently desired to kill Jouralmon for vengeance of the past; but it actually resolved itself down to a case of self-defense; he had been shot at, and he finally had to kill or be killed."

Critton sighed.

"It's logical enough. And it alters the case considerably. I'll hate to have to prosecute Gibney for doing it, under the circumstances. Though, with the facts known, he'll probably get off anyway."

Hearle regarded him quizzically.

"You intend to arrest him, then?"

"Well, things being as they are, it will be more or less of a mere formality, of course—"

"You think he's guilty?"

Critton stared in amazement.

"Hasn't that been proved conclusively enough?" he demanded.

But before Hearle could answer, there came a knock at the door, and Gibney himself stood there.

"You asked me to come here, Mr. Critton," he said. "What can I do for you?"

"Well, I—I found out that you had also come to town today, and so I—I took that liberty." Critton was actually stammering in his embarass-

ment. "I—we wanted to ask you a few questions."
He looked appealingly at Hearle.

"You've been investigating my record, and have
found out about my trips to town in an airplane,
at night," Gibney said calmly. "Is that it?"

"That's it," agreed Hearle. "I know, of course,
that they had no connection with this case. But
if you could tell us what you were doing, it would
serve to ease Critton's mind."

"You know that?" demanded Gibney, in some
surprise. "I was of the opinion that you would be
convinced that I was guilty."

"You couldn't be," Hearle said simply. "Things
don't fit together." He waited, patiently. Gibney
shook his head.

"I was congratulating myself that I had a perfect
alibi," he declared. "For, in studying the matter
over, it looked to me as though I would have need
of it. You rather disappoint me now. Well, I'll
tell you the why of those night air trips. They're
nothing to be ashamed of.

"About a dozen years ago, in Africa, I had a few
adventures, in company with a friend. He saved
my life a couple of times, and we got to think a
lot of each other. Then, in the way such things
have of happening, we lost touch with each other,
until recently. He had lately been taken to one of
the local hospitals here. Last week, he was a very
sick man, and it appeared doubtful for a while,
whether he could pull through or not. When I
first heard of it, late on Tuesday afternoon, I immediately called up McClusky and had him bring
me in to town, because that was a lot quicker than
with a car. Since I was busy all day Wednesday,

233

with Mr. Leadley being out at the ranch, I couldn't very well get away again until Wednesday evening. Having known how it would be, I had already made arrangements with McClusky to repeat the process. After that, my friend was sufficiently recovered and no more night trips were necessary."

"I'm glad to hear that he is better," said Hearle. "That will be all, then, I think. And I'm sorry that it has been necessary to trouble you."

"Not at all," Gibney returned, and took his leave.

Critton stared after his vanishing figure in bewilderment.

"Should I call up the hospital and verify it?" he asked.

Hearle shook his head.

"No need of that. As I said before, he couldn't be guilty anyway."

"Then, in Heaven's name, who is?" demanded Critton. "It seems to me that we have exhausted every possibility."

"Not quite," Hearle sighed wearily. "You are learning a few things, Critton, but still I am disappointed in you. After so much discussion as we have had in regard to alley mud, to say nothing of shoes, I would think that you would observe shoes a little more—especially as you took a couple of sample tracks in the mud, of the man who killed Jouralmon."

"But I thought all along that those tracks belonged to Gibney."

"Yes, you were firmly convinced of it, so forgot to think about the matter at all. Jumping at conclusions is dangerous. As a matter of fact, if

234

you will consider it, Gibney is a small man, and he has small feet. A glance at his feet and at those same shoe prints would have shown you that he could not possibly have made those tracks. They were made by a man with larger feet."

"By Jove, I am dumb."

"Not dumb, careless. Furthermore, as I think I indicated at the time—at least, I made a mental note of it—one shoe print of those in the mud, showed that the right shoe sole was worn—it had a hole nearly, if not quite, through the outer sole. Gibney always wears boots, and they are always in good shape. He is a man inevitably careful in dress, down to the last detail, wherever he goes. The materials may be low-priced, but they are always good. Being a soldier of fortune, he values his appearance, and rightly so.

"The man who made those foot prints, on the other hand, does not often have the opportunity to get into old clothes. When he does, he likes to have them old and comfortable. Being a man of affluence, he can afford to dress as poorly as he pleases on occasion, and such things do not worry him as they would Gibney.

"But as soon as he came to Helena, several hours ago, he went to a cobbler and had those same shoes re-soled. He realized that they might tell a tale, and he did not make the mistake of throwing them away as they were. With new half-soles— but I will let him speak for himself. Wait here, please, a few minutes, while I get him."

Hearle went out. Presently he returned, accom-

panied by Senator Ferguson. Critton's eyes dropped
to the Senator's shoes. But they were a reasonably
new pair with no signs of having been recently re-
soled.

CHAPTER XXVIII

"The Senator, very properly," Hearle explained to Critton, an amused twinkle in his eyes, "has changed his shoes." He turned back to Ferguson. "Our Prosecutor, Van Horn, desires for you to explain why you found it necessary to kill Jouralmon."

Senator Ferguson stared at Hearle for a long moment in silence, his face almost expressionless. Finally he extended his hand, almost hesitatingly.

"So, you—you have recognized me finally, have you, Hearle?"

Hearle grasped the extended hand, shook it heartily.

"Those whiskers, coupled with your name, position, and the years, were a most complete disguise," he confessed. "It took me a long time. Only a combination of events which would convince even a blind man, finally led me to the truth."

"I was rather well pleased with myself, when I saw that I had fooled you," the Senator confessed. "I did want to recall myself to you, but I dared not. When I discovered that my brother had been murdered, and that you were working on the case— well, it seemed to me that the only thing for me to do was to go on as I had been doing."

237

"I understand," Hearle agreed. "I have here," he added, "a letter which your brother wrote to you, on the eve of his death. I just happened to run on it not long ago."

He drew out the letter from Richard Sargent, passed it over. The Senator, with a deep show of emotion on his usually placid features, drew out and adjusted a pair of spectacles, settled into a chair, and read it carefully. Critton watched in silence.

"Poor Dick," the Senator commented, when he had finished reading. "And you worked things out from that letter?"

"Partly," nodded Hearle. "Partly from many other things, of course. What Miss Dixon told me helped, and then too, I had memories of the case. I began to understand the other day, when I mistook Miss Sargent for one of your own daughters. There had been something familiar about her all along, that I could not quite place— her resemblance to the Van Horns, as I remembered them from knowing you. Then, later, I saw that your daughters, Joan, and Dolores Dixon, were inevitably all related, all with Van Horn blood in their veins. With the other things, that made it clear."

"And you want my story," nodded the Senator. "Though I imagine that you have fitted most of it together already. As you know, Dick and I were never satisfied with what seemed to be the facts regarding our sister's death—that she and her husband had been murdered by thugs merely for the purpose of robbery. So we each took one of the daggers that were in their bodies, to be used, once we met up with whoever was guilty, as a warning and an explanation for what we were going to do in turn. But for doing the actual work of justice on the murderer, we each secured another dagger—the two being exactly alike, also. And we pledged each other to devote our lives to seeing justice done.

"Since we would be greatly handicapped by our own names, or by working together, we changed our names, have lived apart, almost as strangers. I decided that I could work best by attaining a position of power and influence in this country. In the attaining of that, I have become United States Senator, and that position has helped to open gates to me—often in far places, where I have traveled when I had the time.

"Dick devoted all of his time to travel. We have always sought the proof that they were murdered by Tinley—or Jouralmon. It was a long quest, to find the actual wielders of the weapons, to get the proof. But we completed the chain of evidence, down to the last proven link, between us. Always we strove to find our niece, Dolores Dixon, to locate Jouralmon. It wasn't the money that we cared about—we wanted to see our niece properly cared for, and justice meted out to the slayer of our sister.

"Dick found Dolores a few years ago, satisfied himself concerning her, but left things as they were, for obvious reasons. She was then in a position where he could not help her in any way, though he helped her indirectly, through her husband. We never managed to catch up with Jouralmon until very recently. Of that, you know most of the

239

details. Even Dick, knowing as much as he did, was not certain that Jouralmon was Tinley.

"I arrived here to find that Jouralmon had recognized Dick, and of course he knew that to maintain his own safety, Dick must be done away with. With the help of his servants, he had succeeded in his purpose. I recognized Jouralmon as soon as I saw him, but he did not recognize me. I was determined, however, to see that justice was done to him.

"And then, at the ranch, it came to me that he knew me at last. When he recognized me, I do not know——"

"I think that I can tell you," Hearle interrupted. "It was on the first Sunday out there. Jouralmon and I had just returned from Helena, and you and Gibney were going fishing. Either the old clothes that you wore, or something, showed you up in a familiar light to Jouralmon. I didn't know what had terrified him, at the time, but it was quite plainly the knowledge that Senator Ferguson was a Van Horn."

"Doubtless. Well, I discovered, from little things, that he knew me. That warned me. I had come, of course, equipped with those two daggers that I had for nearly two decades, because I knew that he was in this country. I realized that, having gone so far along the path of crime already, that he would murder me at the first opportunity. So I was very much alert at all times. Even then, he very nearly got me, in a most ingenious fashion.

"I had been fishing along the lake, and was coming through the woods, staring back to the cabins. I heard no sound at all, but something like

240

a bullet plunked into the tree beside my head, missing me by a scant fraction of an inch. Even then, knowing that he was shooting at me, I kept my head. I moved back, being careful not to betray the fact that I knew he was after me. Leaving my hat for a decoy, I discovered him, came up behind him.

"He had a fiendish little gun camouflaged as a fishing rod, and was waiting for another shot at me. Years ago, I had practiced the art of throwing knives, until I had attained a considerable proficiency in it. I threw the dagger that had pierced my sister's heart, so that it struck in the tree in front of him, on a level with his eyes. He saw it, and understood.

"Even then, taking a chance that I did not know what his fish pole was, he tried, very casually, to swing it about for a quick shot at me. He was clever as the devil himself, and very nearly as swift as a striking snake. I had been debating with myself if it would not be better to take him in a prisoner, turn him over to the courts of justice. I was sure that I could prove him guilty, and see him hang, with your help, Hearle. And in my latter years I have rather gotten away from my old blood-thirsty ideas of justice, have come to rely more on due process of law.

"But I had no choice in the matter. Seeing what he was up to, I had just time, to save my life, to throw the other dagger. He had not turned, you understand—his back was still to me. He was too clever for that. So my dagger took him in the back, pierced to his heart."

Senator Ferguson ended very simply, sat staring

241

at the letter which he still held in his hand. A trace of moisture appeared in his eyes.

"Poor Dick," he murmered. "If I had only known in time, I would have left everything in Washington, have come out as I had first planned to do. But we never know. At any rate, you are all avenged at last."

He folded the letter up, and placed it in his pocket. Briskly then, he turned to Critton.

"You are the prosecutor in charge of this case," he said. "I will waive Senatorial immunity from arrest, of course."

But Critton shook his head.

"I wouldn't think of arresting you, knowing the facts of the case," he declared. "With self-defense, you would of course get off without any question. Even if there was no question of self-defense, why— I wouldn't consider it anyway. He got only what was coming to him, and while I'm sworn to uphold the law—justice too, is supposed to be a paramount duty of my office. As a Senator, you are a leading figure, a credit to the country. Far be it from me to cast any taint upon your reputation."

"Thank you," said Ferguson. "For my own sake, it wouldn't matter so much. I have accomplished what I dedicated my life to. But there are my daughters." He fell silent.

Critton turned to Hearle.

"That letter of Sargent's, addressed to Crusoe," he said. "That convinced me that Gibney must be the man. Didn't it confuse you?"

"A little, yes," agreed Hearle. "But the facts

disproved its being Gibney. And other men could have the same nickname."

Ferguson glanced up.

"Why, Gibney was telling that the other day, wasn't he? But that was what Dick always called me as a boy," he explained. "It was never used, however, except between ourselves, in strict privacy. I called him Robinson, not so much from Robinson Crusoe, as from Swiss Family Robinson. Travel, adventure in far places, always had a lure for us boys. And that lure, at least, was abundantly fulfilled in life."

"One thing more," said Critton. "I can understand most of it—why Sargent was killed, and how. Jouralmon and his servants attended to that. And the subsequent events are clear enough. But what connection did John Kasmin have with the case? Why was he killed?"

"That must have been between himself and Jouralmon," Ferguson said thoughtfully. "I haven't the faintest idea."

"But we have found no possible motive for Jouralmon to want Kasmin killed," Critton protested. He turned to Hearle. "Have you any idea on the subject at all?"

"It was all very simple, really," Hearle explained. "I had it straight in my mind some time ago, although subsequent events occasionally tended to throw doubt on my deductions. But with other things cleared up, there can be no doubt that my first theory was the correct one.

"If you will recall the seating arrangement that night, Kasmin was seated at one end of the table, on the side. Sargent was seated at the opposite corner from him, on the side at the other end.

"Gage, when he brought his movie camera in, first experimented with it at a point behind and between Dolores Dixon and Kasmin. He did not like the effect, so moved it to the opposite corner of the room, between Sargent and myself.

"Yamamoto of course, was supposed to kill Sargent with his own dagger. He knew just what was going to take place in the room, was familiar with it all, seating arrangement included. He looked in when Gage was first setting up his camera, between Kasmin and Miss Dixon. Evidently he did not know that Gage had changed the camera to the opposite end of the room, a little later.

"As soon as Gage switched off the lights, Yamamoto, who was standing by the main switch off the hall, immediately turned that off. Then you will recall, he had to walk for some distance down the hall, in the pitch blackness, to the door of the room. When he came in there, he secured his bearings by the clicking of the automatic movie camera—a slight sound, but plainly audible. He believed it to be between Kasmin and Dolores Dixon. Accordingly, to kill Sargent, he must go to the chair at the opposite end and side, from Kasmin. He went first to the camera itself, taking the flashlight that Gage had, so that it could not be used. It was easy, in the darkness, and not knowing that the camera had been moved, to make the mistake. He moved the proper distance, to the opposite side, and killed John Kasmin, under the impression that he was murdering Richard Sargent.

'If the camera had not first been set up at the other end of the room, or had not subsequently been moved, Kasmin would not have been killed. Jouralmon, of course, knew all about what was going on. That explained his nervousness when the lights were out, his kicking Mrs. Reid—twitching ligaments. He, of course, did not know that Yamamoto had failed to see the camera moved the second time. When the lights went on, he was looking across at Richard Sargent, expecting to see him dead. It must have been a shock to him to discover Sargent alive and well. The camera records his expression when he discovred that Kasmin had been killed by mistake.

"His expression first gave me the proper clue, and the rest was easy to work out, when I remembered the clicking of the camera, and that it had been moved. Then too, Jouralmon's insistence, at the dinner that night, that he had never been in China—that, subsequently, made me suspicious of him."

It was a month later that Hearle received a letter from Joan Sargent, which caused him considerable pleasure.

"Lon and I want you to be a guest at our wedding," it ran. "It will be just a little family group, with my cousins present—the Fergusons, and the Pinards. Mrs. Reid will be present, too. And we all feel that you should be there. It wouldn't be complete without you. And the Senator says there are a lot of old happenings that he wants a chance to talk over with you. Will you come?"

245

Hearle, addressing his own reflection in the mirror, smiled.

"The answer, my dear, is yes," he murmured. "It is something to have my one blotted record wiped clean—and it is something more to have friends."

(The End)

www.ingramcontent.com/pod-product-compliance
Lightning Source LLC
Chambersburg PA
CBHW022013010726
47494CB00003B/1018